Westward

by

Rick Ridgeway

Of all those who are under,

Many are looking over

Their shoulder, although it is only one leap

To beyond-reason gold, only one

Breath to the sun's great city.

All ages of mankind unite

Where it is dark enough.

—James Dickey, "The Common Grave"

1
Cleveland

OCEAN AND SEA

We are all born equal: slushed from a broken bloody womb, crying as our mothers cry, in pain and amazement. Here I am in my sticky caul, slathered with her blood, connected by a gut-like cord. It's snipped, and I'm tugged away. I'm held aloft, gloved hands probing my mucky skin. I'm whacked and scraped clean and turned in an arc in the arctic hospital light, like a skinned seal. My first feeling must be fear. I'm squinting through blooding eyelids at the strange people in the chlorophyll-green gowns. I'm nearly blind, and raw, and lost. This can't be my world, can never be my home.

My memories are like sea water. I loll in my swaddling clothes, crying or cooing or choking. Besmirched, then cleansed. Hungry, then fed. My mouth is made to grasp a nipple, and it's more than hunger—it's desperation. There may be worlds where the newborn and their mothers stay in an endless warm darkness, like a dream, and the babies suckle through millenia and into infinity. That may be the ideal world or the embryonic world or just the dream world, but sometimes, when we loll and dream without language or clear images, it must be the world that our dreams inhabit.

So to pass through infanthood is to feel this dream break over and over and over to wake, wet and afraid and fretful. To reach. To wriggle. To crawl, finally. To blurt some funny syllables. To toddle, tip, topple.

Then to go out into the huge world. Say it's a warm May day, and the grass is a vivid green, and blown bright matter wings at me on the breeze. I try to grasp everything, ricocheting off a tree trunk, trundling over mashed weeds, skidding on the edge of a rain puddle. My bare knee smarts where the hard tree bark has skinned it. My mother skitters around and beside me, exalting with me, rediscovering wind, sun, grass. She is utterly empathic, always. When I am tired and I stumble and I lay kicking in the sweet grass, my mother's there to lift me up. On the porch stoop my grandmother sits, watching us. She wears a white blouse with an oval broach at her neck, a heavy skirt as of many layers of black crepe, and high-topped, heavy black, old lady's shoes.

The keenest memory: I am five or six, and my parents have taken me to a roadhouse, and it's past midnight. My father Kenny has led me to the bathroom, and I've peed strenuously into a big trough that has a row of camphor-scented pucks and licks of water purling along its bed. Kenny has to boost me up so that my shoes balance on the enamel lip of the trough, and I pee downward.

He guides me back to our booth. It has a tawn leatherette hide that squeaks when I sink onto it. I lay facing outward, toward the state. Lights blaze, making my tired eyes ache, but I have to keep watching. I hear for the coolness and softness of my bed, but we can't leave or home yet. I recognize the music. It's a blues song, with a dirty, thumping bass, and nonchalant guitar fills, and the drums and cymbals making their racket. When my mother leans in to sing, her voice is electronically altered, harsher than her spoken voice, pleading and shredding a little. Our booth is off to the edge, but canted toward the microphone, and I can peer directly at my mother. Her wrists are shaking. Her voice is a broken tirade, pitched against the musicians. The words are distorted, but I can pick up a few—"He never could, he never will / But I love him, I love him still."

I can smell the bitter beer that Kenny is drinking. Usually he plays guitar alongside my mother, but the house guitarist dislikes Kenny and won't relinquish his spot. It's painful to watch my mother. I shut my eyes at last. When the song ends, there's sparse applause, a few hoots that aren't quite jeers, and much communal rustling. A man with an oily ducktail strolls out and readjusts the microphone stand, as my mother stands off to the side, fiddling with the bracelet on her wrist. Another singer, short and rotund, her breasts pressed upward in her tight yellow dress, sashays to the mic. My mother bumps down the side steps, her high heels clattering, and walks to our booth.

I shut my eyes again and feign sleep, but when she hovers over me I have to peek. She's smiling. Her lips are quivering. There are hot tears lensed over her eyes. As she lifts me up and cradles me, my insides break and gush and mix, and a tear of urine drips into my underwear. I can smell lipstick, whiskey vapors, perfume, skin and salt—and that salt is the very seawater that buoys all my memories, perpetual and warm and breaking inside me like a contained wave.

In his awkward, laconic way, Kenny tries to comfort mother, but she makes a small sound in her throat, not a word but just an emotional noise, and we weave through the tables, and pass from the hot, smoky, claustral air of the roadhouse to the freezing air of the parking lot. Light snow is flurrying and dancing. It muffles the crunch of the gravel and the metallic peeling of the car door that comes unstuck with difficulty, and then I'm asleep on my mother's lap, in the cool womb of the car, dreamily aware of the thwacking of the windshield wipers as they slash the sliding snow. I can re-member the name of the town where the roadhouse was—Paines-ville. All the way home, I slept curled on my mother's lap, and in my dream I was closer yet, unborn and swaying warmly behind her belly, fed by her sea-salt blood.

Later, when I was ten years old and my parents had left me in the care of my grandmother Eva, the old woman took me to meet her priest, whom she herself did not trust and visited rarely. Agi-tated by my disobedience, Eva wanted the priest to startle me, to un-hex me.

His name was Father Kerensky. Threateningly, he bent toward me, his head big and lopsided, half-shiny and half-dull, with crusts of dirty-white hair and an inflamed-pink, bald center. His bulus bloodshot nose throbbed, tusks of hair curling onto the septum. He breathed on me, a sulfurous snort. I concentrated on not flinching.

Without hesitation he said to me, "Boy, if you pray and pray and pray, and do what your grandma tells you, you will go to heav-en with the angels. If you do not, if you defy her, if you sass and kick your feet on the furniture and pout, very bad things will hap-pen. So." He prodded my knee with his hard, horny finger, and I gazed directly at him. My heart shuddered like a punching bag, but I didn't flinch noticeable. I glared at him, hatefully, and I may have let the beginning of a smile widen my lips. Certainly I had an unhappy ten-year-old boy's capacity for malice.

"You will be a lizard-devil, a pitchfork-sticker, a burning devil boy. Like the black ones over on the east side say, 'Burn, baby, burn.' Like them black boys gonna do, God will do you. Your soul will go up in stinking foul smoke, poosh." He jabbed my knee again. "Forever, boy. Forever. Never—gonna—stop—burning." And he dented my knee with four punctuating jabs. "No good, boy. No good for God or you or your poor grandma or anybody else. You go and read your Bible, and pray, and listen to what your grandma says, and e good now. Go. Get out. I eat my lunch now."

An incongruously pretty lady, pink-cheeked and maybe blushing, her chestnut hair in a thick bun, nudged into the room. She carried the priest's meal on a tray, and he was already fastening a big read napkin to his collar with a tie pin. My heart vibrating, I touched Father Kerensky's large, knobby knee with my fingertip, and said, smiling, "Thank you." I was giddy with insolence, and I let my smile broaden.

"Get out."

I had heard lurid speeches before—playground bullies threatening castration; my grandmother threatening to scorch my arm with a hot iron; a policeman on a horse, once, threatening to trample my skinny ass if I didn't hop back onto the curb. Now this priest with his hellfire vaudeville. What a skulking melodramatic bastard! And what a heavy style: his fouled-snow hair, his tumid beak, his black gunfighter's outfit, his fat black shoes and transparent black socks pierced by his ankle hairs like insect feelers.

I hated Father Kerensky, and the hatred felt tonic. To fear him was to shrink; to hate him was to expand. When I was ten, love puzzled me. I craved it, but it withdrew, divagated, or failed to emerge at all. But hatred. Hatred. Sometimes when it knelled in my blood, when my grandmother Eva acted hatefully toward me, my heart resisted it—the black adrenaline rush of hatred. But what if hatred, seething hatred, were the fuel that drove the engine of life? Perhaps the world pulsed, in its heart, with hatred. Like gouts of hot black blood, or black lava erupting.

The world was fixed in many sets of oppositions. Sizzling inside you were the twin impulses to stop and go; strike and retract; expand and contract; feel and go numb. You could love, kiss, caress, sink in a deep pool of gentleness, or you could hate, sneer, withdraw, and plot a war where the flesh of your enemies would be pounded like veal on a butcher block. You could seek to understand the world or founder in ignorance. You could scale a high hill, your muscles aching in satisfaction, or you could stay forever on the flatland, sluggish and ignoble. You could feed the stray dog or you could harry it from your land, waving a stick and yelling. You could weep for the pain of the world or accept that awful pain as easily as a stem or a pebble or a tear of rain seeping down window glass. You could be a savior or a monster. In dizzying profusion, you could act in all these ways, be all these creatures. Maybe God, so difficult to fathom, suffered this form of warring confusion. Maybe he was hooked up to receive the impulses of the maniacs and the saints, because he had to love them all, accept them all. Some of his children were so beastly, so irrational, so disobedient, that maybe God was overtaxed.

And so He was no help to human beings. That's how I felt, and why I distrusted prayer. I would no more heed Father Karensky's advice than I would rub lye in my eyes. But at ten I had no counter-religion, no surety. At times I felt dangerous and inscrutable, too, even to myself. Alone in my bed, with the metallic taste of my own saliva, and the shifting of my own sapped limbs (for I had run and jumped and lurched my arms on the twilight streets), I could be the scariest stranger, or the most seductive stranger, even to myself.

I longed to lash out at my grandmother, to hit her. When I recoiled from her gruff discipline—her clawlike touch pulling on the skin of my upper arm, her habit of marching me by goading me in the small of the back, her insistence on gouging a warm washcloth into my face when I came inside soiled from play or mischief—I hated her to the depths of her niggardly and foul soul, and I couldn't believe that her soul was immortal. Whatever fire awaited me, the disobedient boy, at whatever unimaginable terminus of existence, she'd burn like a bird impaled on a spit, her face melted to a skull and then her skull charred to a cinder and then that cinder crumbled like dust falling into ultimate darkness. My grandmother would be a firebird.

So I left the feasting priest and the pretty, embarrassed facto-tum, and returned to the ante-room of the rectory, where pamphlets were arrayed on the glass-topped mahogany table, and a dull ivory statue of the virgin stood yellowing, and potted waxy plants tock the furry dust-motes on their dark-green leaves. My grandmother squirmed sideways and then up, digging her cane into the rug. "So?" She pinched my elbow, kneading a little skin around the knob.

I waggled my elbow. "So—I listened. Let go."

As we trudged home, for I had to trudge to stay exactly even with Eva on the uphill sidewalk, I tried to envision heaven and hell. Again my heart clenched and unclenched and knocked like an ex-tra tiny heart in my left ear. I didn't fear hell; I feared earth, even as I loved it. This house, this neighborhood, these people—there were devils enough close by.

I feared, too, that my destination was not the calm ocean of souls, far from the fire, that soughed and swayed in heaven; but the black inward sea, so black that my blood and heart and love couldn't color it, without shores or bottom, the black sea of pri-vacy and aloneness. It was where I lived, inside myself, when my mother wasn't nearby.

It rained after dark, and I fell asleep with the sound of falling, spattering, soaking water, and I dreamt a water-dream.

In my dream my mother floated toward me on the still water that was as warm as tears and that buoyed us both, for it was the water of my inner sea and so exactly at blood temperature, and she cried my name, "Joseph, Joseph, Joe," but I kept quiet, so dark and concealed and mistrustful, bobbing in the warm darkness and resisting my mother's cries, even as my heart leapt toward her as it must in empathy. I fought and fought, my muscles pulling, to wake, but I slept and remained mute. I saw her hair in the gloom, and the anguish in her eyes, blazing in the dark as expressive eyes must blaze, lit from their own mysterious source so that all creatures in the vicinity can read the emotion in them. But with all the force of my divided self, and with all the force of my hannering blood, I clenced myself from her. I shrank into my own hot heart that drummed the tribal song of my own lost tribe, motherless and hateful and inscrutable to myself, and I watched her sail by.

IN THE HOUSE OF LEOS AND EVA

The way to grandmother's house was uphill: past the factories, past the taverns that served the workers as field hospitals serve the wounded in war, past the grocery store with its amber tubing and banks of fruit crates on the sidewalk. In the twilight I walked up the tree-lined hill where Indians once hunted, when Lake Erie was pure blue and Canada beyond was a dense forest growing north-ward to cold infinity.

I passed old dark-skinned trees, maples and oaks and elms and walnuts with wrinkled musty nuts spilled in the grass below and willows with long lashing tails of leaves, pasted on the sidewalk and faded chrome-yellow by the drilling rain. Puddles brimmed where the cement broke into jagged bowls. I sang to myself, broken fragments of a song.

Each house in the uphill corridor was lit by yellow lamplight or gray-blue shuddering TV light, and each had a narrow border of split, clammy cement, or earth, separating it from the next prop-erty. Clogging these three-foot-wide borderstrips were trashcans, rakes, and red wagons. A running child or fleeing felon had to hur-dle it all as he barreled up the alley. The houses were once painted cream or lemon-yellow or chocolate or dove-gray or evergreen, but most became soot-stained and weather-corroded so that their colors dulled to a brownish-gray, as if earth and ash and tendrils of a storm sky had been brewed as a house paint.

Far below, the factories dominated the lakeside plain. Sometimes an aperture permitted a cauldron, or furnace, to flare its devilish fire. Firebirds again. It was as if the factories beckoned inexorably: this is where you'll toil on earth, next to the awesome fire, and this is where you'll go after your earthly toil, into the awesome fre. Some factory workers had smoke, Apache skin, and deep crinkles under their eyes from squinting at the flame. I'd seen them.

Coming up the hill, I spoke to myself: "Now look. Look." When I looked, I saw heaps of smoke rising and spreading in the evening air. If rain clouds drifted down from heaven, factories sent their poison clouds upward, and in West Cleveland the cloud banks clashed into one vast storm front, and quick spurts of fire from the tall brick stacks pierced the updrifting clouds like torches in a dream. More soaring firebirds.

I kept going. High above the industrial flats, the narrow streets on my neighborhood branched and forked, and some had beautiful names, like Iroquois Lane or Lost Nation Road, but my street had a simpler name. It was called Weir Avenue; a weir was a small dam made of twigs, and I like the odd, curt sound of it. I veered onto the smashed, jigsaw sidewalk and scuffed along, booting a tricycle aside and stumbling. My toe throbbed. I embraced a sampling whose base was protected by a tin shield. I spun around it, booting a dent into the tin. Almost home, I stopped to behind me. The sky was heliotrope-purple, and pulsing softly.

High up here, in these battered houses, the workers lived, drank, quarreled, and expired—eventually cooled like the cinders that are the final proof of the smelting process. Several tiers below, the neon tavern signs burned blue and crimson and amber.

In 1952, when my mother was twelve, some oaf beat my grandfather to death with a pipe behind one of those taverns. It was a hut-shaped tavern named Tubby's, and there were damp curds of sawdust on the floor and a glossie of Billy Conn tucked into the mirror frame and an OUT OF ORDER sign tacked permanently to the one unisex john. Who knows where the bartender went to take a leak? But I pondered the alley battlezone many times, and it's not hard to imagine the pissy sod, the drumlike cans full of old punctured tomato juice cans and broken bits of brown beer bottles and wet bar napkins, the coal chips and chunks of gray stone that resemble colorless coral. Easier yet to imagine the boasting, the venomous curses, the excitement and terror of a fight to the death, both combatants greased by an evening's worth of beer and a lifetime's worth of impacted wrath. According to witnesses, it was over quick. My grandfather's blood trickled from his ears as the hot star in his brain died, and two drunks, unable to lift him, dragged him by his ankles over the alley grit and propped him on the sidewalk against Tubby's facade for the police to examine. The killer, who squatted in the alley licking his bloody teeth and gurgling, was tried for manslaughter, eventually, and sent to Columbus to serve a few years. Eva sat in the courtroom and muttered to herself, listening to the bum's testimony.

The house that my grandmother inherited had been her domian, her sanctuary, or her place of incarceration since 1936. That's when Leos married her and purchased the shabby house for $2,800, which was all he gad. Pig-killing money, some poker winnings, goon wages from his bygone Chicago days. The dents and swells in Leos's big pink knuckles equalled coinage and bills.

When I moved in there with my mother, the original furniture still filled the small rooms. Like the exterior colors of the house, the furniture hues blended—plum and violet rugs, rose-pink and oxblood chairs, the dark-tan sofa with its itchy woolen nubs. Age

12

stewed these colors into a brown-gray-dried blood mixture. Dust fuzzed every surface, no matter how often Eva clobbered the fabrics or geigered along with her fat silver vacuum.

For the last twenty-five years of her life, Eva sat in these rooms—cooking, sewing, scrubbing, ironing, listening to the Czech language radio station. And oh Christ, she was steeped in fatalistic dreariness, and she wouldn't listen, wouldn't change, wouldn't even learn many of the English words for what ailed her. She never owned a television, though sometimes she went next door to hobnob with her crony, Mrs. Syzmanski. They sat and drank tea with lemon and watched the flickering gray images on Mrs. Syzmanski's squat little set and clucked back and forth like sympathetic chickens.

But the phantoms of television or movies or the world itself barely impinged on Eva's consciousness. Permanently, she was tuned to her own network, her ceaseless repays of grudge and woe and bitterness. I had little sympathy for her unhappiness; she seemed to generate and exude it from within.

Landlocked in West Cleveland, Eva was kept morose by memories of her drunken husband. Leos was a hatchet of a man—a survivor of the Chicago slums; club fights; slaughterhouses where beeves came bellowing down conveyor belts, their ankles looped, to be clouted, cut, split, scalded, beheaded. There were bins of hacked cattle heads, and small boys retrieved what was usable from the black noses and thick pink tongues and webby pink gums. Marbled white fat accumulated on the floors like beds of sponge, and bigger boys came with scrapers and buckets and mops to pry it loose and swab the sticky slaughterhouse floor. After years of this work, maybe the fires in the mills seemed cleansing to Leos.

Possibly, he came to Cleveland on the train, and he was beaten by years of bloody pummeling, and so ready to take any sort of wife, short and sour-smelling, tall and frail, fat and yeasty and dull. Someone who's always there when you take off your pants and burrow into your bed at night. Possibly, he was the only man who ever possessed Eva, breathed her breath, shaped himself to her in the dark as people must, like pieces of a fleshy puzzle fitted together without volition, guided by God or nature or the tides of a moon that floated billions of miles beyond the reach of the most powerful telescope.

I couldn't understand Eva, as smart as I was and as fierce as my imagination was. What did she feel, in her own bed at night, just before sleep soaked into her? What did she remember? What made her so hateful? I tried to ghost back to Eva's childhood. A hut with a mud yard where chickens pecked and scampered fatly and had spats. Small girls in babushkas, arrayed around a huge black washtub where sour clothes boiled in blue-white sudsy water. One of eight sisters and certainly not the prettiest, Eva must've felt sisterly resentment. Her body was jug-shaped, stubby—her contours ruined any chance of gratefulness. She was pallid. She had opaque black eyes, like melted tar. When she smiled, she looked spooked, pained. If she had a peaked black hat, she could pass for a witch.

Eva was forsaken. When my mother wasn't with me, I felt forsaken, too, but I could caper and dance and chant language like incantations or beseechments or just sheer persiflage, whereas Eva moved slowly and never twirled and was trapped in her few scraps of guttural English, without eloquence or zest or anyone to champion her. So, even as I felt unhappy and forsaken, I was fortunate compared to Eva, and I grieved a little for her, grudgingly.

I remember Eva flaring once, clutching a memory. She was talking to my Aunt Hana, who had driven from Pittsburgh to visit. "Dey come wid swords. Da soldiers. In da yard was two lambs, mama's lambs. You vas little—four, five. They cut dem both up. ook da meat from dem lambs. Da chops. On da ground dey left da innards and t'ings. Dey vore—vat?—dey vore gray coats wid da

14

red ribbons. Mama said, vhen dey go, she said, 'Too bad da lambs, but coulda been all of us'." Eva snorted. "Could be us, too, she vas saying. She seen dat. Vhen she vas a tiny girl. She don't forget dat." They drank their tea.

I strained my imagination tracing my own lineage, Eva and Leos making my mother, my mother and Kenny making me. Why Eva married Leos—what convulsions of the spirit and flesh wedded them together—not even God the puzzle-fitter could explain. When I stood on the porch and beheld the smoking plain, the dark lake lapping in from Canada, the skyline of Cleveland ablaze, I knew that God couldn't explain any of it. It had swarmed out of control, burst the waterline and flooded free, long ago. I felt my persistent doubt, that God was tiny and afraid and weary and drifting in the dark Himself, watching the celestial skyline and the far lakes of space and the fires of other processes that lit the farthest reaches of space and matter.

Defying Father Kerensky, I kept my Bible, velvety brown and with scarlet waxy coating on the page rims, in the drawer with two old valentines, a small blue cap, and a broken yoyo.

No, the Bible couldn't aid me in fathoming Leos. I knew this much: that from 1937, when he was fired at the foundry, until his death by alley misadventure, my grandfather Leos took a two-wheeler from the loading dock every Friday afternoon and wheeled it to the beverage store and bought two cases of beer and wheeled them home up the hill, bumping along the root-pierced and uneven sidewalks. The sonofabitch drank at least forty-eight bottles of beer a week for fifteen years, and I doubt that one swig ever lightened his heart, or made him hum a melody, or reminisce, or look into the sunset and imagine himself as a patch of fading reddened sky.

Yet he must've had notions—to live, toyer, to make a child with Eva, to work diligently, to eke out some small happiness. He must've dreamt of being a child sometimes. A child with warm slobber on his chin, waiting for his mother to return and coax him to smile, to tickle him where he was most tender, to sing to him perhaps. Toward the end, when he went looking for fights, everything he ever wanted or experienced must've been smelted to a black residue at the bottom of his memories. Home from work, his muscles aching, bereft inside himself, he sat and drank and drank and drank, until he ventured out one night to seek the company of other bitter sots and was pounded dead.

I saw his gravestone once, a small chalk-white rectangle with his name and dates in indigo intaglio. Brown leaves were threaded into the rough grass that grew against the stone. Eva knelt and attacked the grass, yanking it loose in clumps and crumbling the friable dead leaves. She brushed the exposed earth with a whisk broom and whisked the gravestone. Then she did something that only she would do: she bent lower, as if to kiss the soil, and dribbled saliva on the earth-darkened stone, and polished it with the sleeve of her black dress.

LANDSLIDE

Behind Eva's house the landscape formed a steep earthen cliff, and down the cliffside over the years a gradual lava of trash crept. On the road above my grandmother's property people stopped and poured out their junk—a broken stove where mice came to live, an enamel cabinet, a vacuum cleaner with a hose like a baby elephant's trunk, boxes of smashed dishes, rags and clothes (including a bloody polka-dot dress), organic garbage that attracted vermin. Once, on a quiet evening, I sat on the back stoop and suddenly a tire rolled crashing down the hillside, hit a tree, and spun to a stop.

Bits of odd color showed through the foliage. A garden of discards grew, and was always in season, gleaming even in winter when the sun melted the snow and emblazoned the polished surfaces of things. A big red chair with burst wadding sat against a sapling, and the sinking sun lit it like a smoldering throne. Shards of bottle-green and lavender and opaque-white glass reflected the light. Old rags sank into the earth like sopped medallions, their wrinkled ridges frosted with soot.

The breeze carried spoiled egg smells, rust smells, and one spring the unmistakable scent of decaying flesh. I clambered up the bank and found a dead dog, a spaniel with outsized furry brown ears. Someone had pitched him from a car, or he had straggled there to die in a nest of leaf mulch and small twigs; I never heard him whine or cry. I dug a cranny for him and dusted him with lime and tamped him beneath the earth, as mucus ran from my nose and my eyes bled hot fluid.

Grandmother fussed about the yard, the stoops, the broken sidewalk in front of the house. I had to scour and clean and rake and tend every square foot of it; she'd smack me if I defied her. Being touched by her always repelled me. I sensed that she didn't want to handle me; that she considered me, in the twistings and turnings of her bitter mind, obstreperous, uncontrollable, bad. And so, with my own mean, vengeful child's logic, I often wanted to be bad. I'd tamper with her food, rearrange the slits in her bed frame so that the springs would buckle, hide her sewing needles, futz with her radio so that it was set to a loud rock 'n' roll station. She'd stalk me, chopping at me with her swollen old hands whose knuckles were chunks of gristle and whose skin was like rendered, brown-tinged animal fat webbed over the bones. A hag's hands.

Up close, her onion-and-gravy breath was strong. Her harsh English was naturally nagging, digging. She had no gentleness, no grace, no serenity. Sometimes I seethed wordlessly, unable to defend myself or phrase an argument that she could understand. Being stymied like this made me hate her, inside and out. I hated her shoes, clumpy and black and clodhopping, and even said it out loud once, laughing at the absurdity of it as I blurted the words, "I hate your shoes, too."

"Vat's wrong vid my shoes? Christ in heaven!" And she clumped after me, knocking me on the back and shoulders with he ugly hands.

I hid in my room. I tried to see my situation as a comedy, and I tried to empathize with unhappy old Eva, but I couldn't contain my simmering hatred. Hunkered on my bed, I formed the words: "If you hate everything so much, grandma, why don't you die? Crawl in a hole and die, like the dog on the hill. Or hobble down to Republic Steel, climb the catwalk, and cannonball into the vat Do something completely insane and awful. I can go over to Mrs. Syzmanski's and watch you on the evening news; you'd make an ingot. Mrs. Syzmanski could cluck and sniffle and roll goobers in her big old nose, and then she'd probably give me a plate of molasses cookies and a glass of milk. Maybe she'd adopt me. At least she wears house slippers instead of those goddamn Russian army black clodhumpers you wear. If it's that miserable to be an old lady, just jump into the fire. It's the only way you'll ever be noticed or remembered. Kamizake grandma." But I could never say this spiel out loud. Eva would whack me, and as much as I wanted to hit her back, I couldn't.

It was written in my blood: never hit a woman. Even Leos hadn't. He sulked and brooded and sat in a beer stupor, but he held his violence for outsiders. He discharged it in taverns, attacking men like himself, soul-dead drinkers with foam on their pepper-colored mustaches. Spasms.

It was endlessly hurtful, and impossible to expunge from my mind. I was like a paper link in the chains that we made at elementary school. Each link was a grievance: Eva despised me because her sisters shunned her, Leos neglected her, Karin (my mother) disobeyed and disrespected her; and when my mother fled to Chicago, I was left behind like an eyesore trunk or an uncomfortable chair in her house, and she clumped around me, bickering and chafing, maybe thinking that I belonged on the hillside with the other debris. There were times, alone in the darkness of my room, where her sewing machine was kept on a card table, and where her plastic garment bags filled two thirds of my closet, that I lost the surety of my sustaining hatred and my self began to shred and dissolve, and

I lost the hope of seeing my mother again, of feeling her pressed to me, and I felt that I belonged to the rubble-strewn hillside, too, and I wept like an animal into my mashed pillow to muffle the noise, for there's nothing more noisome than the sound of crying and the enjambment of fluid in your eyes and nose, and I hated myself for weeping.

THE SCHOOLYARD

School was no better than home. My teachers were mostly un-trustworthy, and some displayed a bitter obdurateness similar to my grandmother's. Miss Tull—with her equine face, thin wormy lips, rumpled handkerchief crammed into the folded arm of her sweater, eyeglasses on a chain (squinting, she groped for the chain, as the class malignly tittered)—was typical. She exuded distaste for her job. She relished any opportunity to mete out punishment. One day, I sat by the window, listening dully to Miss Tull lecture about Andrew Jackson, and someone set abuzz a model plane in the ad-jacent field. I swiveled and peered through the dusty pale-green glass toward the spiraling plane. Miss Tull strode over instantly and smacked my knuckles with a plastic triangle.

The playground was a fire-zone of hostility. I knew a few other kids in a desultory way, but had no skill in making friends. I was afraid to share my unhappiness; afraid to be rejected as an unhap-py freak, abandoned and living with a hag grandma. And I didn't trust the form that adolescent friendship seemed to take—the silly whispering, the tickling and gouging and ragging, the forming of devilish pacts where two or three boys would gang up on a loner and bully him. I feared these situations myself, but I was desperate to conquer my fear, because fear could swallow you like quicksand. The truly afraid didn't even need to be picked on; they existed in a constant state of incipient panic.

Anyone who provoked me was in for a battle. I'd seen fights where kids ripped each other's belts off, tearing the loops on their trousers; kicked and bit and dug their fingernails into each other's faces; fought until they salivated; screamed until their voices went hoarse. Childhood could be a vicious folly.

The older kids hogged the swings and athletic equipment, and the first and second graders idled or found sticks and rocks to mess with.

A pig-tailed girl ran a stick through a mud puddle. Her knees were white and irregular from roller skating scars and healed nicks. She reached under her dress with one hand to tug her underpants. She challenged me with her oily-brown eyes, her flared nostrils. "Who you lookin' at, Seymour? Your name Seymour Butts?"

"Wouldn't wanna see yours."

"Oh yeah. You ain't got enough money, honey." She dredged her stick through the muddy water, spattering my pantscruffs.

"Stupid."

"Have some poop soup." She flogged the puddle, getting herself muddy up to the rim of her skirt.

"Stupid." I walked away, my heart thumping. I couldn't fight a girl.

"Stupid cupid pooped his toopid," she teased. Her name was Dot.

Two boys, Frank and Anthony, found a frog at the swampy edge of the playground. They squashed it with rocks. Where its rubbery skin was torn, it leaked a gelatinous syrup darker than human blood.

"Dare you to eats the feets, Joe," Frank said.

22

I stood watching them. Trying to get someone to sniff or lick or swallow some disgusting item was an obsession in the schoolyard. Frequently, kids were dirty little ghouls.

Frank lobbed the torn frog at my feet. "C'mon. Ain't chu hungry today, Joe? Joe the whizbang math kid. Seven times seven is forty seven helpings of guts. Good for ya, too."

"You can't even multiply. You eat it—maybe it'll make you smarter." I toed the frog on its pale, split belly.

"Fucka-you-mama, I ain't gonna eats it." Frank capered, making moronic grimaces at Anthony, who was the appreciative second banana in their bully team. "Give da Kingfish some bread dere, so's he can slaps up a samwich, An-tunny." Frank did a Mardi Gras strut, to match his Negro dialect. Mocking Negroes was popular at our segregated school.

Anthony took a sandwich in wax paper from his bib overalls, and peeled the sticky halves apart. Chortling roughly and flaunting his smeared tongue, he licked jelly from the bread.

"Save the goop to stick it on with, idjit. Joe wants a jellyfrog samwich. Here." Frank snatched the bread and used it like mitts to clamp and lift the frog. "If you don't eat your lunch, Joe, Joe-Blow, Joe-Blow-Me, me an' Anthony'll stomp you shitless."

It was late March. My face and hands were chilled, but inside I steamed. So many situations in life felt ambiguous, unsolvable, but in this trap I felt definite. These two slugs, taller and heavier than I, could not defeat me.

I poked Frank's face. I felt the wet underside of his lip. His teeth gnashed as I ripped at his mug. He bit the rind of my hand between my little finger and wrist. I hit him as hard as I could with my left fist. When he keeled over, discarding the frog sandwich, I kicked him. The rubber toe of my tennis shoe, stained with a dab of frog entrails, vibrated Frank's ribs. He bleated.

Anthony rammed me and threw me sideways. In the mud we

thrashed and scratched and pounded at each other. I rolled onto Frank, and as I gouged at Anthony's wincing face I ratcheted my elbow into Frank's belly. A grove of legs and trucks sprang up around us, and one kid counted from one to ten as I spread eagled Anthony and slapped his nose bloody.

The recess monitor, a big penguin of a teacher in a black rain-coat whose name I didn't know, pulled me off Anthony. Frank lay fetally, clutching his sore ribs. My knuckles were skinned and my lip bloody. Neither Frank nor Anthony had landed a blow on my face; I must've bit it myself during the fracas.

My grandmother had no telephone or car, so I was driven home and delivered to her, by a custodian in gray coveralls who kept kidding me and calling me "Sonny Liston." Eva listened to the cus-todian's laconic account of the fight, then shooed me inside. As I took off my muddy clothes, she stood in the bathroom doorway and squawked at me.

"I ache too bad. I don't vhip you right now. Not today but someday soon you gonna get a vallop." She gave me a baleful look. "You vait."

I kept fighting, though. I fought until the damnable kids left me alone. I didn't unbend and seek friendships, but a few classmates congratulated me on my prowess as a fighter, and I joshed imper-sonally with them. My grandmother obliged on her threat. She hit me with a belt, caned my legs, beat my ass awkwardly with a cropped old bed slat, even washed my mouth out once with Palmo-live soap when I sassed her obscenely. She used anything she could wield, swing, or jam in my rattrap mouth. Not often, but when her anger peaked.

I accepted the blue-yellow-lavender bruises as part of my skin. It was only my youthful skin; I would grow older, stronger. My own anger outweighed hers; which was why I never dared to wing back. In time Eva would die and rot in her coffin, and her last shreds of skin would cling to her brittle bones, and from the dust-and-bone remains her long white hair, unbound, would push like roots through the rotting wood of her cheap coffin. Moles would tramp through the dirty twinings of her hair and worms would wriggle through the dashed wood and live inside what was left of her, and everyone alive above ground would forget old Eva, or if they remembered her at all their memories would be contaminated by hatred of her.

When I mused in this way, I knew that I was partially wrong; that I antagonized Eva sometimes; that I never spoke kindly to her; that the hatred, given space to expand, could fill me and corrode me. I pulled back from the brink of hatred. I pinched myself, slugged myself, warned myself to stop. I thought about my mother, and a heat that was the opposite of hatred spread like a balm inside me. I knew what the word "hypocrite" meant, and I didn't want to be one. I didn't want to be infected by the hatefulness that I saw so frequently in the faces of schoolkids, adults, teachers.

So often I had to recoil from myself. Often I must look exactly as they do—malignant, clotted, senseless. In the oval mirror in my room I studied my visage—dark, deep-brown eyes; dark-pink lips, obstinately set; wavy brown hair that swept over my ears; olive skin, like my mother's. Kenny was Polish-Czech and my mother was Hungarian-Czech, yet I looked more Italian than Central European, and I was a bit scary even to myself. I frowned, winced, set my lips more tenderly, tried to smile, smiled at last.

"I'll hawker in your gravy," I threatened Eva, sotto voce. My breastbone thrummed with silent mirth.

Down the hallway, Eva rustled. Her bed springs squeaked as she shifted like a nesting bird. I turned off my bed lamp and climbed into the cool bed and sifted down toward sleep. Eva's snores were faraway, as were the nighttime rattlings of distant cars and the wail of a train, borne mournfully away toward Pennsylvania, and I sifted further down, like gentian drops in a deep beaker of water—blue, blue ladders of liquid collapsing toward the bottom—and I prayed not to be a hater, and I slept in the place of sleep where my blood didn't pound but only murmured.

MOTHER IN FLIGHT

My mother came home for a year, leaving Kenny to scrounge on his own in Chicago. It was 1968, the year of the assassinations, and we went next door to watch Robert Kennedy's funeral cortege on TV. White horses pranced and soldiers marched in a slow parade and people along the route waved, wept, stood stunned, embraced. My mother sat on the rug behind me and embraced me, too, and caressed me absently, as if the motion of the caress could prevent the taint of distant death from soaking into my skin.

"Dey shootin' ever'body," Mrs. Syzmanski said. "What dey should … dey should drop dis guy wid da gun in boilin' hot water … teach da guy some manners."

I winced and snorted softly. My mother hugged me tighter, conveying her disapproval of Mrs. Syzmanski's boneheadedness. We had a physical telepathy, and the hug said: "Only Doris Syzmanski could see murder as a crisis in manners, to be solved with a sadistic scalding. And look, Eva's agreeing with her; she's clucking like a hen." Mother kissed my ear, nibbled it playfully. I smiled and squirmed a little, gooseflesh zigzagging across my breast.

"What chu—eat his souse?" Mrs. Syzmanski chuckled. She served tea and angel wings, fragile cookies like honeycombs dusted with powdered sugar. As delicious as they tasted, it felt strange to be eating as we watched the images of grief and leave-taking. Testy, combative, energetic Bobby Kennedy was dead, and we sat, not awestruck but nibbling cookies. Both my mother and I licked our fingers and sipped our hot, tannic tea, leaving the majority of the cookies for the old ladies.

All summer and into the fall, my mother fought with Eva, who nagged at her compulsively. "So put da boy to bed." I was not "Joe," but "da boy"—a counterweight yanked back and forth on the pulleys of their lifelong argument. Mother despised her job at Higbee's, a huge fortress of a department store that sat beneath the spire of the Terminal Tower. She sold handbags, then jewelry, then books. She brought home *Life on the Mississippi*, *Of Mice and Men*, and *Winesburg, Ohio*, which I kept in my room to read when I was a little older.

The night that mother fled, it was snowing. Snow blew up on the porch and made a dune against the milk bottle locker. Mother stomped inside, wearing red pumps and a beige dress and black nylons and a red cloth coat and a conical cotton snow-hat the same blonde shade as her hair. When she stood on the mat, shaking her hair, her whole body crackled with cold electricity. Her car heater was on the fritz and she'd misplaced her gloves; she seized my warm hands and twined her cool fingers around mine and warmed herself. She bent and kissed the crown of my head.

Eva sat in her big faded-red chair, the lamplight shining on her deeply wrinkled, yellowed-ivory face. She had a sock on a wooden darning egg, needling a hole shut. "Shut da door."

Mother banged the door shut, rocking the dishes in the big cabinet of glass and vermillion wood. There were dragons etched into the wood, and they flourished their tails and spread their wings

28

and gnashed at each other eternally.

"I quit," Mother said. She faced Eva directly.

Eva pricked her needle into the taut sock, a blue one of mine. "So dat ain't news. Vhere you gonna get some money at now? Go mooch on Ruby an' dem, you don't like it here."

Ruby was Kenny's mother. She lived about five miles away, but she and Eva disdained each other, battling like dragons whenever they met. Ruby was shrewd and had no illusions about Kenny, yet she defended him, perversely, to spite Eva. Lacking sufficient English or patience or tolerance, Eva would swell like an iguana and lash out at everyone. I secretly like Ruby; I admired her gumption.

Mother didn't start arguing with Eva immediately. We sat at the dining room table and ate lentil soup. Mother buttered bits of bread for me and fed them to me with her fingers. I smiled and munched, preferring simple bread to the thick, gray, garlicky soup.

"Sewer stew, for me and you," Mother joked, making a face as she spooned up some soup. She was smiling, too, a pinkness in her cheeks. She had beautiful green eyes. Lagoon-green, Kenny called them; they were actually gray-green, though not murky as I'd imagine a lagoon to be.

I formed a question, but it snagged on my heart and then in my throat. I swallowed my bread, then spoke softly. "Can I go with you? When you leave."

"I haven't decided to leave, honey. It's that joooobbb." She moaned the word, trying to be comical, but I could read the unhappiness in her eyes, which always revealed her feelings. Mother laughed helplessly, and said, "They hired this big nasty Brunhilde of a floorwalker. Oh, Joe. She accused me of swiping twenty bucks. I'd like to steal twenty bucks —or two thousand bucks, if I could get away with it. But I probably just gave the wrong change. Twice to be off by twenty. I can never get my register to balance. I think one of the other girls might hit the No Sale key on my register, and steal from me. We're all broke. I hate to even accuse anybody, but I know I didn't take it. They were nasty about even giving me my last measly check. Nobody should have to work at that awful shithole." Mother had a spasm of laughter. "Everybody hates their job, Joe. We'll have to get you violin lessons or make you a pilot or a forest ranger or a doctor. Anything but sales clerk. Half the girls at Higbee's are ready to go on the rampage." She cuffed my face, gently. She let out a long phhewww, her lipsticked lips bowing.

I went to bed at eleven o'clock, and as I lay sleepless I could hear Eva arguing, cajoling, thumping her chair. My mother hissed back at her, pleaded, attacked. Then I heard my mother's shoes clatter across the squeaky boards of the dining room floor. The swift, jangling noise, so different from my grandmother's slow, pressing tread, sent a shiver of sensation through me. I listened intently.

Next door, the suitcase thumped to the floor. Mother was packing. The china cabinet jiggled. I felt a hot urge to pee, but I stayed in the sanctuary of my bed. The warm liquid shifting inside me intensified, and I felt ready to sweat, cry, piss, dissolve.

Mother came into my room. Her name was Katrinka, but she had shortened it long ago, in defiance, to Karin. At the peak of their argument, Eva had barked "Katrinka," and the name was sliding on the fluid inside me.

"Joe?"

I was afraid to answer. I smelled her skin, her dress, her breath. I wanted to burrow into her, to feel her soft sink in the closest, most shocking way. I stayed still.

"Joe? Talk to me, honey. I see your eyes."

I lay cocked on my elbow, facing her face. She crouched by the bed, gracefully.

"Slide over so I can sit by you, honey."

I scrunched toward the wall on my narrow bed. Mother sank onto the blanket. More of her scent, so fragrant, was released from her dress as she settled. I wasn't old enough yet to understand sex, but I felt an overpoweringly sexual love for my mother at that moment, and surely, without knowing what was happening, I would have undressed her and kissed, stroked, sucked, somehow plunged into her on the peg of my boy's penis, if only she'd shown the slightest sign of permitting it.

When she stroked my hair, my scalp prickled. I felt an intolerable emotion, a volcano of animal love and unhappiness and futility spewing heat over my heart. As I wept, so my mother wept. Certainly she felt the same heat. As she smoothed my hair and made sounds of comfort through her tears, I forced myself to stop sniffling.

I listened to her. "Nooo." (Clotted still, all the o's coming out her nose rather than her throat.) It's oh-kaaay." (Cracked, helpless.) "Honey." (That one sweet word, clearly enunciated.) Mother embraced my shoulders as I lifted myself a little from my furrow. She rocked me. Her heels raked the bare floor as she lifted her legs and sprawled against me. Light from the hallway made her visible from the neck up, and in the neckline of her beige dress a tiny freckle pulsed, where the cords of her slender neck strained. She had unpinned her honey-blonde hair, and soft tendrils swing loose as she wiped her eyes with a handkerchief and wiped mine, too.

I saw her kissing my father Kenny once, and it awed me. He was like a reluctant king being crowned, somehow resisting her kiss. Yet she pressed into him, gripped his waist, and lifted her body on tiptoes to kiss him fiercely. "Jesus, Karin," he said. "Take it easy." She kept her head against his chest for a moment longer. When she withdrew, her face was steeped in hurt, shock, pleading. It was Christmas Eve, and I was four or five. There was icy slush outside, and the agonized revving of cars trying to find traction.

My mother softly thumbed the wet skin beneath my eyes. Her hands were warm now; arguments, sadness, going away—they could throw some heat. She made a nervous sobbing laugh. "You still have the bird book I gave you?"

Where my tears had dried, there were salt encrustations. I was fretful. "Yeah."

"Chickadees and hummingbirds and mourning doves, hmmm? You learned 'em all. What was that you asked me one time? You were so concerned about the birds...'Where do the birds go during a hurricane?'... And I didn't know what to say. Mothers have to fake it a lot of the time, Joe. I'll tell you that secret. And I just said—what?—that they fly above it, I guess. They just outfly the big wind...I don't know if that's true, but I was thinking about it before. When we were crying."

She sat upright. Bending down, she kissed me on the shoulder, and I was scalded with feeling again. I had to squeeze my kidneys, clench my bowels, will my heart not to explode.

"You were right before, honey. I can't fool you. I have to leave tonight. I'm going back to Chicago to look for Kenny...Damn him. If I didn't love him, I'd really want to trounce him." She shook her head, trying to laugh it off. Kenny was fragile, and she probably could best him in a tussle. "I'd take you, honey, but I'm so close to broke. And your schoolwork'd get all messed up. It's better if you stay here. Look at me, Joe. Listen."

I had turned toward the wall, despairing. Gently, with one hand, mother eased me around.

"She can't help it, Joe—the way she is. None of us can—much. It's aggravating...it's hard to accept...it's heartbreaking sometimes. But it's the way it is. I'll tell you how I feel about mama. I know that she gave birth to me. She breastfed me. She changed my poopy diapers. She took care of me and clothed me and loved me as much as she could—but it's all snapped since I grew up. Everybody's disappointed her. Daddy did, I did, Kenny did. There's not a single thing in the world I can talk about with mama in a civil way. She hates music, she hates car rides, she hates men. She's—"

My mother went silent, groping for language. I could hear the old icebox rattle in the kitchen, and then a dog yowling faraway. "She's sad, Joe. That's the thing. Christ knows, I need comfort, you need comfort. I know you do, honey." Under the blanket she clasped my hand. "I ache when I'm away from you. If only I could arrange it so that...Oh, Joe. She needs comfort, and there's nobody to give it to her. I can't even when I try. She won't accept it. I don't know if she could accept it from anybody...Try not to hate her or fight with her. Please." Mother squeezed my other hand, too.

When she took her suitcase and garment bag to the living room, I ducked into the bathroom to pee and wash my face and blow my nose. Eva's bedroom was dark, but I could hear her rustiling. When I went to the foyer, where Eva's galoshes sat on the mat, mother had already stored her bags in the back seat and started the engine of her old brown Pontiac. The shafts of headlight illumination held swarming snowflakes, as if they were a movie projector and the night sky were the screen.

Mother clattered back up onto the porch and into the foyer, which smelled of stale air and mud on the treads of the mat. She hugged me and kissed my lips, and it was the last kiss I got from any woman until I was nineteen and rolling loose in the world.

SUMMER AT RUBY'S

My grandmother Ruby's house roasted in the summer sun. Sleepy flies fizzed in the window, their shadows shaking on the amber window shade. My thumb fit exactly in the loop at the end of the cord. When I tugged the shade up a few inches, a fly tumbled down and alighted on the ledge. I pinged it with my finger and it looped aloft, uninjured.

"Crank the shade down and go outside." Bluish cigarette smoke hung in the air around Ruby's head. I yanked the shade level with the sill, and the room was dim again. Every July afternoon was like a warm coma, and I had no words to justify my incessant fiddling and no one to associate with and nowhere vital to go.

I made a circuit of the yard, kicking softly at the edges of things. I was ornery enough to kick a dog; boredom and cruelty were intimately connected, but knowing this didn't stymie my urge to kick. The yard was littered with unattractive and uninteresting booty. Ruby's husband, Luther, prowled the West Side neighborhoods in his bandit truck, swiping aluminum lawn chairs, a recliner, rakes and hoes, a lawn mower, a rotted sandbox, some tomato plants.

Along the back margin of sun-scorched lawn, a ruined wire fence sagged; its posts were askew, and thick weeds clotted the fallen mesh. In an oak tree purple-black grackles, as shiny as gasoline, sat and squawked. Just to relieve their ugly boredom, they flew to another tree. If they were thirsty, Luther's scalloped, cobalt-blue birdbath couldn't service them, because Luther, drunk, had chipped a wedge off it with a shovel; it couldn't hold water.

I felt a surge of angry energy. I rambled into the field beyond the fallen fence. Nettles grazed my cuffs and burrs snagged on my knee; I dug them off and crumbled them. Across the field, where sumac and elderberries grew, the railroad tracks glittered like hot dimes. Up the tracks rumbled a long train with drab-maroon and peeling-gray boxcars. It made the air reek like a gun battle. A forlorn sentry in a striped cap stood on the caboose platform and watched the tracks recede. I made a shooting noise in my mouth, shhppurnggg, and imagined the caboose-keeper sailing off his perch like a human grackle.

I edged along the swampy lowlands by the tracks. A water-snake lived in a trench, swimming over submerged cinders. My guts jumped at the alien snaking motion, then digested the sensation. The snake was sinuous and beautiful, or sinister and ugly—I couldn't decide. I couldn't imagine, quite, grabbing him from his channel and lifting him like a whip. His flat head squirmed into the air and pivoted, scoping me out; then he went gracefully back under.

I was determined to grab something. I found a fat frog, its skin mottled and brackish, its eyes dimmer than the snake's malign, alert eyes. When I lifted it up, the frog pumped and struggled like a heart. I let him hop free. I stood in the soaking heat, and when I rubbed the rail with my shoe it still sizzled from the train's passing. Where the sunlight hit the long bed of cinders and coal chips, they dazzled like dark gems. I picked up a chunk of coal and skimmed it into the marsh. The water where the snake swam burbled and ran into the weeds, but the marsh, dead still, smelled like rot, like death.

Circling back to Ruby's I crossed an area of marshed weeds; perhaps beasts scrimmaged there nocturnally. There was a deeper depression nearby—a grave-like patch that breathed cool air, as if from a refrigerator deep in the earth. I pictured a vast, cold nest of snakes, wriggling in a underground cavern. My skin prickled, and I ran home like a shot. I was eleven years old that summer.

Ruby kept her spot in the living room all day long; it was like a vigil. She read Louis L'Amour westerns and murder mysteries and *The Chapman Report* and *Hawaii* by James Michener, but mostly she watched movies on television. She sat in a yellowish-tan chair that was the color and texture of pigskin gloves; she squared a beach towel over the cushion so that her rump wouldn't stick to the surface in the clammy heat. Next to the chair was an urn-like ashtray with a metal scoop the size of a hubcap to grind her butts in. She smoked Pall Malls. She fanned herself with a Japanese wicker fan decorated with pastel waterfowl.

Ruby snorted at the TV commercials, constantly vilifying the carpet hawkers and strident car salesmen who dithered in four-minute blocks. When the movie returned, the black-and-white-and-gray images absorbed her; at least they didn't displease her, as the actions of living beings often did.

Warm-blooded, Ruby wore short-sleeved cotton or rayon blouses. Her upper arms were plump and pink, and her vaccination mark made a bump like a flattened wad of bubblegum on her bicep. Too proud to expose her veiny, heavy legs and outsized feet, she usually wore white slacks and slippers with corsage-like puffs of imitation fur.

Her hair was thick, wiry, dirty-silver, suety where some white showed—combed back in a gush so that her ears were bared, their rims crimson. Ruby wasn't precisely mean, but she threatened meanness. I translated her characteristic gaze as, "I'm not mad at you yet. But I could get mad." But I could get mad." Herr eyes expressed cauterized sorrow, and vengefulness. Still, she was easier than Eva to live with; she owned a TV and a truck and a .22 pistol.

"What are you up to now, shitheel?"

"Nothin'. I'm just sittin' here. It's too hot to stay outside." I never knew whether to call her "Ruby" or "grandma" or "ma'am." Being impersonal felt awkward; but Luther never called Ruby by name or endearment or nickname or imprecation, either. She was so formidable that no one could address her casually.

"When the movie's on, don't kick the floor. When it's this damn hot, stay still. You might live longer."

"Who's gonna kill me? Jeez, I was just shifting around a little."

"Keep it in idle" She coughed out a gout of smoke.

I put my hands on my hot knees and willed my feet not to wriggle or grind. At age eleven most kids have a Mexican jumping bean or lurch-mechanism implanted in their bones and innards.

We watched an old gangster movie, *The Roaring Twenties*. Belligerent James Cagney tickled me, and the actresses were as odd as dolls in their antique hair-dos and silver dresses. Sweat spread in the crevices behind my knees, but I didn't squirm. When the commercial popped up, I hummed an old song that my mother had practiced once, "Twilight Time."

Ruby gazed at me with her stone-gray eyes, but made no complaint aloud.

RAIN SKY

In August my mother and Kenny were still stuck in Chicago. Kenny was emptying wastebaskets at Chess Records and dealing dime bags of marijuana. My mother was singing in clubs for a pittance, barely enough to broker Kenny's drug deals. On bad days, or days when he didn't want to waste shoe leather, or days when the haze of city heat laid everybody low, Kenny probably lay prone on the bed and listened to the radio and smoked his own stash. He was the opposite of a good capitalist.

Kenny called to borrow money, and Ruby spat the word "Borrow" back at him. No one could express gall and exasperation more vividly than Ruby. She didn't care if I heard her berating my father; she wasn't callous necessarily, just non-protective. I imagined Kenny's comebacks—his drawled excuses, his promises, his serpentine pleas. Kenny leaked failure like a scent—a skunk trail of thwarted deals, squashed ambitions, void schemes. Yet my mother continued to love him—like oxygen, blood, motion

"Studio time! Get serious, Kenneth. You and Karin should move to Keokuk or some place like that. Find a motel to manage. Or a pancake house that'll loan you both aprons." Luther chortled, delicately, so as not to rile Ruby.

Ruby grimaced and lit another cigarette, cradling the phone to her sore-looking ear. As she listened to Kenny's rebuttal, she watched Luther peel a damp label from a beer bottle and paste it on my arm. Kenny's blood father, Gabor, was long gone; peppered in a holdup of a Toledo liquor store in 1959. As shaky and unassertive as Luther was, he'd lasted with Ruby for nearly a decade.

"Well, I appreciate that, Kenneth. You're the love of my life too. What a life." Ruby looked as resolute as an executioner at that moment; she hung up the phone.

"What're you shits lookin' at?" She put her cigarette down and ran her hands through her hair. "There are three boundaries to worldly existence according to Kenneth. Death, taxes, and Karen's singing career." She lipped her cigarette and exhaled a cloud of smoke. It dribbled out her nose, shot like steam from a broken gasket out the sides of her mouth, and made a dense, milky-white cloud.

"Joe, I like your mother. I'm on her side. But as far as singing, she might just as well shoot down to Houston and try out for the next unit of astronauts. Then we'd have a rooting interest in outer space. Kenny could call us every week and hit on us for money to buy Karin's spacesuit and helmet and boots. We'd have our own little Peggy Lee in orbit."

"Mother's got no use for Peggy Lee," I ventured, wanting to rile Ruby a little. But she didn't react.

Luther goosed me as a warning, then went to the refrigerator and uncapped another beer. He never contradicted Ruby, never tried to dissuade her from her flights of sarcasm, never voiced any of his own woes. Nor was he ever harsh to me. He just sat and sipped beer placidly, whenever he was home. Fried eggs in the morning, nickel-ante poker in the afternoon, thievery a few nights a week—that was Luther's life. He read fishing magazines, but never fished. He kept his pipe-fitter's union card in a plastic holder in his wallet, but hadn't worked at it in years. He and Ruby rented the house, furnished and utilities paid, and owned nothing but their clothes, their toiletries, their weapons. I never once saw Luther kiss Ruby in the open.

I jammed the damp label into a pellet and dropped it in Ruby's butt-urn. When I went outside, there were lateral grooves of orange sunmelt and ashen rain clouds over Lake Erie. Maybe rain was pelting Canada. Birds trilled a rain-chant in the trees, and the silver-green leaves trembled in the slightest breeze. My heart drummed, and I felt that peculiar combination of restlessness and indecisiveness that was the signature of my boyhood summers. I was like an immature lion—and this yard that I prowled was not my veldt, but my zoo.

I sat on the bald ground by Luther's pilfered and re-planted tomato plants with their clusters of tiny stillborn green balls, and ground my wrists into my eye sockets to blot the hot salt tears that stung and rainbowed. I hated the emotionless stasis of summer, and hated even more the emotion that discharged in tears.

Without stating it in words, even silently, I knew that my mother was not a fine singer; that Kenny was a screw up; that my unhappiness showed no sign of cessation. Was there a way to nip unhappiness? Or did you have to be lucky enough to be born to happiness, and to swim with it like a salmon on a long stream that ran from birth to death? I rubbed my eyes some more, not able to form the questions or puzzle out the answers.

I watched it get dark, and the sky was dramatic enough to overrule my own boy's pain. An inky tincture spread from the storm clouds and over spilled the last orange runnel on the horizon. Lake birds flew westward like dark scraps blown from a faraway fire. Those birds might be as ignorant of direction as I was; they could be flying in blind grief or terror.

There was no thunder yet, but my hair and skin tingled. Sometimes I teased myself with a monstrous inner voice, and I began to do it now. "Goooo, boy. You're a lightning rod. A firestack. You'll be nothing but wet cinders if you sit out here. Open your mouth wide and chew your own face. Goooo on."

I pinched my arm. The breeze cooled my skin, riffled my hair, ghosted across my lips like a kiss. Who ever kissed me except for my mother? It wasn't hard to remember and savor those kisses. In memory I held a perfect kiss just then, as the thunder tumbled and bowled over Canada. It was a winter kiss from last year. It was the taste of mint spittle, for my mother had been sucking a peppermint candy, and of fading lipstick from her red lips.

It rained—in spatter, in densely falling drops, in blown sheets. Ruby stood at the back door, yelling at me. But when I came inside, she wasn't angry; she toweled my hair, and gave me a dry shirt, and permitted me to stay up late and watch *The Thing* with her and Luther.

LEE AND BUTCH IN FLIGHT

A few days later, my Aunt Lee, Ruby's daughter, showed up in her rattletrap Dodge, the trunk held closed by twine, pieces of chrome gone, the grille compressed. It was leaking oil smoke, too. Lee had her son Butch with her. She was married to a Seneca Indian, Antonio; Butch was thirteen now, heavyset, with a pink-tan-brick complexion and slicked-back rusty-black hair. Lee herself was a frail redhead with hurt, cedar-brown eyes and the thinnest arms I'd ever seen on an adult woman. She didn't look like she could lift a phonebook.

Lee explained her situation shyly to Ruby, who stood on the porch fanning herself and frowning. Lee said that Antonio was coming out of Attica in a week. She was on the run, and penniless to boot. She'd forfeited her damage deposit; she'd had a yard sale, but some kid had made off with the cigar box full of fives and tens she'd kept on the card table; she'd pawned two rings to raise gas money. Driving from Salamanca, New York to Cleveland, she and Butch had had nothing to eat but packaged lemon pies and a thermos of coffee. Lee had eighty cents left. She showed the three quarters and the nickel to Ruby, who relented and invited them in.

While Ruby made bologna sandwiches and heated some soup, Lee said that Antonio had a load of grievances. She hadn't answered his letters since '66; she claimed that he'd criticized her grammar and spelling. Butch drank a quart of ginger ale straight down and ate four sandwiches, bologna rinds and all.

That evening, Lee sat on the couch and told us more of her saga. Lost jobs, stolen purses, saved money mis-spent on stenography lessons, Butch getting disciplined at school, Butch breaking all of her 45s. Her skinny arms flitted and semaphored as she poured it all out. She kept a balled-up Kleenex in one hand to sop at her wet eyes.

Ruby sat unfazed, sipped red wine and sharing her Pall Malls with Lee, who smoked awkwardly, like a teenager. Butch and I shot marbles on the wood floor, and I was thankful that he didn't try to bully me.

Ruby gave my room to Lee and Butch; Lee took the bed and Butch used an air mattress. I slept on the couch, whose hide stank like dirty laundry and spilled beer. I squirmed and maneuvered in the strange sleeping space, tickling my toes into the cushion, finding the cool velvet-like fabric on the underside of the couch-arm. The refrigerator grunted and vibrated, and the air was still warm at midnight.

Immediately Lee found a job as a waitress. She left for work before first light, her old Dodge punting backfires off the porch and rattling the window frames. Ruby fed cereal to Butch and me every morning and then ejected us. She couldn't tolerate Butch's antics in a tight space. He clodhoppered the floorboards, juggled couch pillow, cursed and burped at the TV.

"Beat it, you two. Go hunt for dinner. Club something to death and drag it home."

"What a scumbunny," Butch said. He did a cartwheel on the lawn, as chunky as he was. He had slipped a dollar from Luther's money clip and nicked four Pall Malls from Ruby's pack, and he chainsmoked these as we ambled past the empty, gutted house next door and the shingle warehouse and the match factory. We went uphill toward the stores. The steep climb made my thighs ache. We could see the luminous lake water and a few yachts.

When we approached an outdoor fruit market, Butch sped past and snatched a grapefruit and an orange so swiftly that the clerk, weighing bananas, didn't even notice him. When I caught up to him a few blocks ahead, he was hunched on a sandstone wall. He gnawed grapefruit pulp and winced at the bitterness.

"Missed out on your half of the orange, boy."

"You stole it, you should get t' eat it. The pink grapefruits are the sweeter ones."

"Yeah, but I got the pissy-colored one. Here ya go, Joe." He gave me a clump of pale grapefruit meat.

"Thanks."

"I wish I had a canna lighter fluid. We could get some hot dogs for lunch. You know those chicken-neck fruits that push the doggie carts? They got tuberculosis 'n' bad posture 'n' shit. They're weak little freaks. Don't scrunch up your face, boy. Listen...When we lived in Buffalo, I used t' go right after 'em. Squirt some lighter fluid on 'em, boy, 'n' threaten t' set 'em on fire 'less they forked over a couple free dogies. 'N' don't hold the sauerkraut, chicken-neck, or I'll make you go whoosh! Toro toro toro! They'd be shakin' 'n' shittin' like chicken. I wouldn't lie."

"You ever really burn one? Just for a hot dog?"

"I ain't tellin'...You be cool and tonight we'll go rockin'."

Butch didn't mean rock and roll' he meant stone-throwing. After dinner, with Luther housebound and nursing a beer, and Lee and Ruby watching a cop show and also sipping beers, we went out in the twilight and up the hill again. The match factory blazed like the Titanic, and through the open windows we could see the conveyor belt conveying a parade of miniature matchboxes. Butch probed the roadside curb and found a few egg-shaped stones, the easiest to pitch.

"I hope you can run good, shortlegs. They never caught me rockin' yet."

"Lee said you got sent away for six months once."

"That was for settin' a fire in a classroom. Nothin' major."

Butch blammed his chest like a gorilla and gonged a rock off the siding of a house. We ran away in the purplish dusk, laughing and snorting. From behind a bush he lobbed a big rock, grenade-like, off the door of a passing car; it made a vicious thunk. We scrambled up an alley, slippery with restaurant garbage, and skidded out onto the sidewalk. Panting a little, we rested beneath an awning opposite a tavern. We weren't too far from Tubby's where my grandfather Leos had died.

"Let's go get some pop." Butch gouged my arm.

The dark, air-conditioned tavern was like an aquarium, with bits of floating gold light like goldfish. I saw that the light came from guttering candles in orange glass candleholders. Along the big mirror behind the ranks of liquor bottles with their nozzled stoppers, there was a long banner of identical black-and-white Rocky Colavito photos. At the bar sat a burly woman, swarthy and pigtailed like an Indian squaw. She wore a sweater to shield her skin from he cool air. She hoisted a fishbowl of beer and drank.

The bartender was disagreeable. "What're you guys, midgets? We can't serve midgets."

Butch sneered. He fished out his stolen dollar. "Give us two orange pops, Papa-OooMau-Mau." The bartender was sallow and squamous and leached-looking; I'd seen his twin at a greasy spoon on Prospect Avenue downtown, spatulating fried potatoes into a mound on the grill. On the bartender's thin arms there were emerald tattoos—they looked like dense ivy.

As she rotated on her leatherette stool to study us, the squaw groaned. Her belly bunched against her buttoned sweater. Her face was scored with dents and scars and notches, like the earth under a rock. "Serve the kids, Herman. You germ. These are my kids. This is Stan, this is Fritzie. Do a trick for Herman, kids." Her lips were plummy, her eyes shining with crapulous sportiveness—pleased by an opportunity to rankle Herman.

"Okay, midgets. That'll be seventy cents. Eighty, counting the deposit, 'cause you ain't drinkin' em in here."

"Keep the change, dribble-lips." Butch slapped the bill on the bar, and handed me my pop. Herman did have thick, saggy, melancholy lips.

"S' long, Hoiman. Next time we kerosene-bomb your scrawny ass," Butch taunted from the doorway. The old Polish squaw laughed as we scrammed. The pop burned in my throat as I swigged it on the run.

On the way home we angled across back lots, scrambling downhill, and threw our empty bottles against a tin shed. A big man in khaki shorts came out of the back door of a house and yelled at us, but we outran him. There was burning sweet citrus phlegm in my throat.

Butch said, "I wish we had slingshots. We could lay across the street for Herman t' leave his joint "n" boink a nice rock off his noggin."

NIGHT VISITOR

Late August. I was on the couch, tilting toward sleep, when the doorknob jiggled. I got up and padded to the porch window. Lit by a streetlamp, a man in a blue shirt and jeans and hightop black tennis shoes stood by the door. He noticed me at the screen and squatted, facing sideways, peering in at me. I could smell his sweat and his sweetish whiskey breath as he spoke, "Good idea if you let me in, fella. I see Lee's Dodge. I know she's here. Otherwise, I'm gonna get up on the roof and do a stomp."

This was Antonio. I could see his vehement dark eyes in the spill of light. Hundreds of bugs bombarded the streetlamp.

"You're not some little orphan Lee's adopted, are ya?"

"I'm Kenny's son—Joe."

"Joe. I'm glad to hear that. How's Lee, Joe? She been slippin' around on me sideways?"

I couldn't answer that. "How'd you get here?" I said, needing to say something.

"Thumbed. Took a bus from Erie to downtown Cleveland—you ever been that bus station over on Chester there, Joe? Felt like homecoming. Every other hanger-on looked like an inmate, and the ticket-sellers looked like screws. Gave me the Four Roses willies. You followin' this?"

"Yeah."

"So I had t' bum fifty cents t' catch the Rapid to West 25th. Then I walked these last couple miles. I'm here—that's the thing. Broke parole like a goddamn recidivist motherfuckin' idiot. But Joe, there's nothing meaner than the terms of a New York state parole. I believe it's a spillover from the Rockefellers. These millionaires make these restrictions that a man just can't live up to. Anybody leavin' Attica should get twenty thousand bucks and a chauffeured limousine and a bottle of champagne on ice. A man's already had his punishment, he doesn't need any Rockefeller parole restrictions. Point is, I got no more use for anything inside the state boundaries of New York. They are the meanest, most unreasonable motherfuckers this side of hell. The Rockefellers wanta yank me back in their godforsaken state, they'll have to call out the dogs." He dug his hands into his thick black pompadour. "I need to see Lee presto. Let me in."

It was a strange, calm conversation. Many things in existence gave me stabs of fear, but not Antonio here. I unlatched the door and he went staggering past me to the kitchen sink and doused his faced and sucked long gulps of water from the tap. He was famished for water.

Antonio took a dish towel and rubbed his face dry. He clenched and unclenched his fists, but he didn't seem angry. I sat on my couch-bed in my skivvies and watched him.

He spoke softly, "So you're Kenny's boy. Goddam." He made a click in the back of his throat. "Everybody in the world's got some jabberin' monkey for a daddy—and you got Kenny. Is your mama pretty?"

"Yeah, she is."

"Figures...Are they here by any chance?"

"Nah. They're in Chicago."

Antonio's eyes flamed. "Which room is Lee in?"

"The one next to the bathroom with the *Visible Man* poster on the door." The poster was Butch's innovation.

"Okay."

"Butch is in there sleeping on the floor. Don't step on him."

Antonio grinned and let a soft, whistling wheeze. "Amazes me that Lee's still drivin' the Dodge. Tell me one thing—she hasn't been trickin'. She'd be drivin' a better car...Well, I been hittin' you with way too many shovelfuls of shit here, Joe. You go back to bed...I'm just a recidivist and I gotta go wake up Lee now and see if she can deal with the reality of me."

Ruby stepped into the hallway, barefoot, her yellowish toes gnarled. She wore a white nightgown. She stood blocking Antonio.

"Antonio, you smell like a plague dog. Go take a shower the very miminum."

"I have to see Lee. She's smelled me before."

"She's not going anywhere with you. You better believe that. Go take a long shower, rinse some of your miseries down the drain. I'll get Lee up."

Antonio made his soft, regretful wheeze. He had an aura of great gentleness. "Who bestowed royal status on you, Ruby? How come I never got wind of it—the coronation and everything? Didn't Luther ever rap you in the chops even once? Or is he, like, your serf?"

"You goddamn baby, Antonio. How'd you make it through five years at Attica?"

"Don't tempt me, Ruby. You don't know anything about Attica. Say two more words about it and see what happens."

"You stink. And I don't see your gun. You wanta threaten me, Luther'll come out here and blow your goddamn head off."

"Let him do it. Just don't give me orders. I'm not doing anything that anybody tells me to do. Never again. I'm a truant-fuck-up-recidivist-Rockefeller-hatin' motherfucker, and that's final."

"You're a dumb Indian thug with delusions of grandeur. You'll be dead before the leaves are off the trees. When you get plugged, don't do it on my property. Now go take a shower."

Antonio wheezed. "Kiss me, Ruby. I haven't been kissed since 1964. I'll take one even from you." He breasted up to her.

Ruby signed. She kissed Antonio on the cheek. She held her arms out ironically, ushering him toward Lee's room.

"There. Queen Ruby gave me a buss."

"Don't press your luck."

Antonio walked past her, not too brazenly, and opened Lee's door and hit the light switch and shut the door softly behind him. Ruby got her cigarettes and plunked herself down in the pig-hide chair.

"Can you believe Luther? He'd sleep through anything...Turn off the kitchen light, Joe."

I obeyed her command, and returned to my mussed bed. I usually didn't ask Ruby questions, but I risked one then.

"What's a recidivist, exactly?"

"It's a helpless case like Antonio who can't learn, doesn't wanta learn, and will never learn a goddamn thing about survival."

"Thanks."

EVERYBODY'S BAD

Over the next week, Luther and Antonio took the truck out every night, scavenging and stealing. They stole tires, batteries, cartons of shirts, a load of canned mushroom caps, empty pop bottles in wooden crates that fetched three dollars a crate. Twice I saw Antonio counting wads of crinkled singles, fives and tens at the kitchen table. As Antonio dealt the bills into piles, Luther watched him cagily, lip-counting. He handed Antonio a wet rag to wipe a grape jelly smear off a bill; Butch liked to lather his toast with grape jelly, and he wasn't always accurate spreading it.

On Labor Day evening, on the eve of my first day in sixth grade, Antonio reeled into the house clutching his torn cheek. Luther came after him, cursing and kicking at the furniture. Antonio had a knife slash seeping blood under his eye. Ruby, muttering her wordless disgust, disinfected and bandaged the wound.

Antonio and Luther sat in the living room drinking rye. In a call-and-response style they maligned the nerve-case cardplayer who'd slit Antonio's face.

"Get it stitched up tomorrow, fool," Ruby said. She took the truck to visit a friend. Any bandito action that Luther and Antonio pulled that night would have to be on foot.

"Maybe I need a good scar, Luther. I wasn't scary enough. A man gets scary enough, he doesn't have to worry about knives anymore. Shit, I knew a few inmates whose faces were so scary that knife metal couldn't even penetrate 'em." Antonio wheezed.

"Year. I seen some of them buggers, too," Luther said.

Lee sidled in from the bathroom and sat on Antonio's lap and traced the shape of the bandage with one slender finger. She cooed to him. She wore a chemise with patterned flamingos, pale-orange and cadmium-gray; the designer didn't know that flamingos were pink, or didn't care.

Antonio hobbyhorsed Lee and gave her a sip of rye, which made her choke. He massaged her back.

"Am I back in your good graces, Lee? Huh?...That's where I canna be. I'm cut, bedraggled, pretty close to tapped out in the wallet, but at least I can be back in Lee's good graces...Right?"

"Yeaaahhh...How deep's this cut? You cut him back?"

"No, I didn't, Lee. I didn't have a chance to."

Lee was pale, haggard, freckle-dusted, loose and woozy from her bath. I think she was taking pills, too. As she nuzzled Antonio, she opened his white shirt and tweaked a tough brown nipple. His chest was coppery and hairless. He smiled as Lee fondled him. Her pale legs, so slender from calf to ankle, jounced as he rocked her.

"Where's Butch at?" A whispery wheeze.

"Took a hike. Maybe he went on melon patrol." Lee giggled. "He's become a pretty good thief. I know you're proud of him."

"Oh, Lee." Antonio let a long sigh of air out. "Hey, Joe?" He looked over at me, his eyes filmed with some murk of pain or consternation. Even so, his face looked noble; it always did. "You're a six grader now, huh?"

I smiled and nodded my head, affirmatively.

"Just remember one thing, Joe. The teachers never mention this." He drank the last sip of rye and squared his shotglass on the coffee table. "Everybody's bad. Right on up to the warden and the governor and the archbishop and the president…You want a different deal, fly to another planet."

Lee wiggled, her arms clutching his torso. "Don't tell him that. Jesus, Antonio." Lightly, she pinched his back.

Antonio broke Lee's grip convulsively and caught her as she spilled backward with his left hand and cocked his right fist and pounded her with a quick punch and her nose burst. Crimson blood gushed out. Lee was gasping and swallowing blood and sneezing. She clutched her face as Antonio held her, tightly.

Luther goggled forward on the couch, rocking like a humpty toy, drunk, his eyes distressed just a little; he said nothing. My heart butted the walls of its containment. I said nothing.

Antonio unfurled a red handkerchief with black dragons woven in a pattern on the red field, and used it to sop Lee's blood. Dandling Lee on his lap, he let her cry herself out.

"You see. I warned you, Lee. I warned Luther here. I warned that goddamn bitch Ruby." He stroked Lee's tresses, which were the color of cedar shavings, and cradled her gently.

It was getting dark in the room, but no cooler. My heart shuddered up into my shoulder and down into my bowels. Antonio kissed Lee on the forehead.

"Get me some ice and a washcloth, Joe." I couldn't fathom Antonio, couldn't forgive him; yet I couldn't help but see the sorrow in his eyes, as clear and unmistakable as the sun or the moon in the darkening room.

THE TWIG INSIDE ME

In November Antonio took $40 from the music box on Lee's dresser and got in Lee's car—as she slept, wheezing softly through her crunched nose—and fled. Two weeks later, the Dodge was found abandoned in a parking lot in Des Moines, Iowa. Antonio had vanished.

Lee rode the bus and the Rapid to work. She saved her tips for a few months, found an apartment to rent near the West Side Market, and moved there with Butch in January. She took a new job at a coffee shop within walking distance, and there were times that she had to carry home greasy sacks of stale cake-donuts, sinkers to make meals for her and Butch. At junior high Butch fell in with the Rack, ducktailed hotheads who preyed on hippies and straight students alike. Butch bragged that he never got a grade higher than a "D' in his life, yet was always passed ahead a grade because his teachers feared him.

I got my old bedroom back for awhile, but in June Ruby sent me back to Eva's. Luther was in jail, pending trial. He'd been caught stealing lumber from a building site. Ruby was sick of the house, the ratty furniture, the smell that drifted in from the tracks and the marsh, the moldering dead-end feel of the neighborhood. She moved into a three-room apartment out in Lorain, where it was quiet and the trains didn't neigh and rumble all night long. When Luther made bail, he came home to an empty house. Stoically, he bunked with a couple of his poker cronies; Ruby wouldn't speak to him, and wouldn't give his truck back, either.

Ruby had some money in the bank, but not enough to keep me around. She treated me kindly in May, when the frogs were peeping in the marsh and the saplings in the field were pale-green, and when she delivered me to Eva's, she hugged me goodbye. I wasn't much of an asset to either woman. Eva's money was dwindling, too.

In September I switched schools, entering junior high. I rode the orange school bus down into the scrubland, a mile from the factories. The school was an imposing fortress—endless rows of olive-green lockers; high-ceilinged classrooms, burnt-brown like sockets in a hive; a gymnasium that stank like a musty hamper; and the swarming, buzzing, stinging students. It was hard to feel human in such a big school, whose corridors echoed with slammed steel, like a prison, and massed footfalls, like a stampede, and massed jeering noise, like the cries of a rioting lynch mob. I didn't like school, and I couldn't imagine anyone liking it.

Yet, I confounded the teachers by excelling at classwork. It's not that I was eager to memorize the dull schoolbooks; it was more that I didn't want to resemble oafs, dunces, louts and truants, who scrambled every day in a monkeyish competition to see who could be dumber, blunter, more disruptive. In seventh grade I began to love language. That summer I had read my paperback dictionary from A to Z, and *Winesburg, Ohio*, and a lot of Steinbeck and Mark Twain and Stephen Crane. I could add and multiply to infinity. I grasped easily the cold particulars of science. I could fill in the countries on a blank globe—Tunisia a divot between Algeria and Libya, Chile like a leech clamped to Argentina, Norway and Sweden a binary horn sprung from the scalp of Finland.

The student groups, cabals and gangs were all clamoring for status. Long hair was permitted, but I kept mine trimmed. My dad Kenny was a hippie of sorts, his hair as long as Eric Clapton's; I distrusted that look instinctively. It seemed wheedling—look how woozy and giggly I am, how cool, how eager to join. As free-spirited and rambling as the hippie tribe pretended to be, I didn't want to join it. Some of the worst suckups, simpletons and drudges gravitated to the hippie bunch, smoked the hippie dope, and rotely learned the hippie lingo. I had to pinch myself at times, because I fulminated silently like Spiro Agnew, that big slick-haired slug. Without bombs or guns or fellow travelers or any kind of game plan, I was an anarchist.

In my friendless, pariah state, I had acquired a reputation for aloofness and danger. I was short but strong. I exercised every night in the basement at home. I did isometrics, pushing like Samson against the stone walls. I lifted Leo's anvil until my biceps throbbed. I reeled off three hundred pushups without strain.

I set my own diet, too. Eva's staples were meat, noodles, gravy, dark bread, and sweet, yeasty pastry. Reluctantly, she bought the fruit, vegetables and cereal that I wanted. Her idea of a vegetable dish was cabbage fried in butter with sliced sausage and red onion; she'd never tasted broccoli in her life.

In seventh and eighth grades there were no enforced recesses. I skipped lunch, spending my free period in the library. I found some Steinbeck that I'd missed—*Burning Bright*, *The Wayward Bus*. I studied pictures of Ceylonese gardens, Incan ruins, the Gobi desert, Civil War battlefields where the sun fermented and exploded the slain soldiers, Turkish poppy fields, African game preserves.

A lion sunning himself in sleepy arrogance reminded me of Robert Mitchum, Ruby's favorite movie star. We'd watched *Out of the Past* one night, and even Luther had stopped diddling his beer bottle and had snapped to attention. Robert the Lion—let someone traipse onto his savannah and try to mess with him. He'd be dead quick.

As I paged through the histories and geographies, earthly images accumulated—heat to bake you, deep water to drown you, animals to gnaw you clean. I seized on the notion of a simpler world—rock, earth, grass, forests, streams, a few singing birds and pollinating insects; no animals and no people. I couldn't inhabit it myself; I'd have to disembody and float through it as a spirit.

Without happiness, without hope of love, human flesh was as useless and homely as a toad's bumpy skin. When my flesh cried for pleasure, the counterweight of unhappiness snuffed the cries. It was as if a voice that ruled the heart of the world spoke back, "You can't have it, can't taste it, can't touch it." When my mother phoned, every few months, and Mrs. Syzmanski gimped across her yard to fetch me, the wright of my unhappiness sometimes blocked my power of speech. I listened to mother's litany of small victories and large defeats, and I could feel, keenly, that she loved me and wanted me with her, but I was balked in sending love outward. As Mrs. Syzmanski knitted a few feet away, I temporized and tried to form the right, magical sentence—and couldn't. I listened to my mother unwind emotionally, lovingly, and at the end of our talk I spoke a blubbered "I love you" and let the connection be severed.

In bed, later, I mulled it over obsessively. Peoria, St Louis, Kansas City—she and Kenny were drifting westward, farther away from me, into unknown territory. Kenny was no less feckless than ever; I knew that he squandered her meager earnings. How could she be happy with him? His latest scam was selling seeds, little packets of seeds, that he kept in the trunk of their car. For a while he'd had the territorial rights to stock vending machines—combs, condoms, SenSen, Kleenex packets—but he'd lost the last few boxes of stuff in a card game.

Eva seemed inured to estrangement, and to the possibility that Karin might never return to claim me. She was becalmed, eating her meals after I'd steamed my vegetables and had my yogurt and cleared out of the kitchen. As long as I did my chores, she didn't bother me.

In September Ruby drove over in Luther's salt-rusted truck and we went to the Rialto, nicknamed the Rathole, to see *Walkabout*. She ducked out into the lobby every twenty minutes to drag on a butt, and we developed a running gag.

Ruby: "What'd I miss?"
Joe: "Nothin'. They're still walin'."

The girl on the walkabout was lovely, more imperious in bearing than my mother but physically similar. When she floated in the oasis pool, it was the first female nudity I'd ever seen. I swooned inside myself and squeezed my knees to stop from shaking. Both a tentacular heat and a chilly fear passed over me. How would I ever approach a beautiful girl and what could I possibly say? What would her eyes express when she beheld me? Merriment? Scorn? Distrust? Could she possibly melt in love as I did?

The greatest mystery: how could I summon what Kenny had in abundance? That sleepy, passive confidence. That slouch and shrug that conveyed an invitation—cling to me, caress me, love me like a female cat arching ecstatically against a texture, her eyes gone cloudy-gold and her belly purring. That perfect feckless inviting coolness.

When Ruby dropped me off, she had a standoff with Eva, who hulked on the porch. Eva wouldn't invite Ruby in. Ruby toed the rubber tread on the top porch. She taunted Eva, "What's the last movie you went to see, Eva? *Gunga Din*?"

Eva shot back at her, "I seen dat circus picture. Back vhen Leos took me. Vadda you care?"

Ruby dug at the rubber cleats with her big foot. To irritate Eva, she lit a cigarette. She rifled her purse and fished up her black velvet change purse and unclasped it and took out a five dollar bill and unfolded it and gave it to me, all the while dribbling smoke up the porch steps toward Eva.

"Ride the bus out some Saturday and see me, Joe. We'll have a beer and watch the bowlers on TV. She winked at me, egging Eva on.

"Thanks".

Seasons passed and I became a Freshman in high school. One day I was walking home from school—in clement weather I avoided the bus, preferring the long uphill solitary trudge—and as I passed a field where some boys were playing football, I heard shoults. "Joe! Hey, Joe! Play with us, Joe! Talk to us, Joe! We're your biggest fans, Joe!"

I recognized the shouter. His name was Danny Trevino. He was thickly muscled, taller than I was, and very aggressive. I had watched him barge into kids in the school corridor, cursing them and provoking melees. I had seen a kid retract his head from a drinking fountain and accidentally brush Trevino, and Trevino had jammed the kid's head back onto the gushing white enamel scoopo and chipped his tooth. I had seen Trevino pin a girl, squirming, again a locker, and feel her breasts through her sweater.

Now Trevino jogged over to the sidewalk. "Don't be such a lame scuzz, Joe. We're gettin' all dirty and snotty out here, and you just flounce by like you're the fuckin' Prom Queen. What gives, Joe? You avoidin' us? Don't play hard t'get, 'cause we can get ya. I heard you were tough, anyway."

He bobbed and weaved, snorting back some mucus. His face was damp from exertion; his short, curly hair a glistening black like sun-struck cinders. "Say somethin', fucknuts. Somethin'." He knobbed a knuckle into my arm. I stood there in my dry clothes, tranced; I knew that it would be folly to run.

"Say, 'Fuck you, Trevino, you big snotbunny. I hate your ass an' I ain't talkin' to you. I'm P. Q. Joe, the Prom Queen, an' I'm just mindin' my p's and q's....' I know you can talk, you little suckass fuck. I hear you in English class. Come down t' the dump some time an' I'll show you much worse rats than that *1984* rat. You ain't seen rats, missy."

I didn't have the words to argue with him. In a crisis, there was a valve inside me that shut off the dumb language of threats, jokes, sarcasm, hyperbole, teasing. I stood there.

"Aww, fuck this. Help me get this guy, Archie." I started to move, but Trevino lunged at me and clutched my arm. His shambling pal, Archie Pollard, took my other arm. As I went rigid in my upper torso, only my heart twisting, they stiff-marched me about fifty yards. There were two apple trees at the edge of the playing field, in the endzone, and some bushes and a big hill of earth where kids rode their bikes. Embedded in the hill were planks, affording the bikers a chute to wheel down.

Six or seven other players tagged along, laughing and encouraging Trevino and Pollard. They flung me down under a tree and bent over me to restrain my arms.

"Let's get his pants off and see what shape his ass is in. Look at these fuckin' pea-green Polack khakis. Get your mama t' buy ya some decent threads, Joe." I felt a shoe on my bare back, where my shirt had slid upward, and cold mud grinding in.

"Lay there and peel for us, fucker. I ain't jokin'." Pollard let my arm go. I yanked free from Trevino, and he lost his balance. I stood up and dodged a few feet away.

"Holy fuckin' mother, that did it. Grab him, Archie."

Pollard darted at me and clubbed me on the shoulder and dug his arm into my midsection. Trevino grasped my legs and tipped me over. As Pollard held me, Trevino loosened my belt, unzipped my pants, and tugged them down until they snagged around my ankles.

"Pull his undies down for me, Archie. I don't wanna touch his ass."

I writhed and strained. My blood rioted. Pollard's fingers pinched my buttocks as he slid my shorts down. He straddled me, keeping one hand firmly on the small of my back and the other, looser and stroking, on my thigh.

"A little white chicken-dick," Trevino guffawed. "Get me somethin' t' do an examination with here. Hey, Toot. Get Doctor Dan a stick so I can do an exam on this nasty little white ass."

A tree branch snapped and a few brown apples tumbled loose. I smelled rotten fruit and trampled grass and raw earth. I smelled Pollard's breath as he loomed over me. Then I felt the twig, sharp. Trevino dug the twig into the opening of my ass. A peeled splinter grazed my scrotum, which prickled and shrank. As Trevino probed the sharp wood into the taut wrinkle of flesh, I clenched and winced. Crying out would make it worse—I swallowed a scream whole. I was nearly still pinned by Pollard, yet my body radiated a helpless titanic resistance from within.

"Open up your ass and say ahhhh. That's it."

Inside me, just a few inches, but jagged, the twig sliced. The pain went up into my guts. I ate another cry, and I could feel the blood breaking inside my mouth where I gnawed myself.

"C'mon, Danny boy. He's startin' t' bleed. Take it out." Pollard withdrew pressure, shimmying both hands mockingly around my waist and then lifting them free. When Trevino pulled the twig out of me, the pain grew worse. My balls ached as if they'd been pulverized. Up in my guts, nausea rolled.

"Good show, Dan-o," Pollard said. He grinned down at me. "Joe here never complained once. He liked it...hey. Hey, Joe. You got potential as as ass-bop. I know some guys on the varsity, real gorillas. I'll tell 'em t' look you up...come on, Joe. Pull your pants on 'n' go home and douche your butt out. Get ready for the next shift...Next time, be nice to us. Maybe we'll let you play stick-fuck with Toot, or Gazingy over there."

The other players hooted and pummeled each other.

"Yeah," Trevino said. "And next time wear a little bit of grease on your miserable ass, Joe. Make it easier for us. Now blow us a kiss and get outta here. Go on."

I pulled my shorts and pants up. I hobbled a few feet. Without warning Pollard rushed at me and kicked me in the lower spine. I pitched forward, my hands splayed against the cool ground. My entire body had a cold, dank film on it; I felt as cold as the autumn earth. Weaponless and without any words, I walked away. A step at a time, I began to absorb the pain. The pain was tiny; my hatred was huge.

At home I went into the bathroom and locked the door and undressed and sat writhing on the commode and strained my guts and bowels. I ejected some bloody waste against the sides of the bowl. With rubbing alcohol I disinfected the torn tissue inside my raped ass. I winced, I whimpered, I sweated cold sweat, I clenched every muscle from my scalp to my heart to the soles of my feet, but I refused to cry. Even though they couldn't hear me, somehow it would complete my enemies' victory if I wept, so I blocked the tears and sat as still as I could with a wad of alcohol-soaked cotton, tinged red with my blood, pressed to my anus, and as my skin gradually grew warm from the heat of the bathroom pipes and my own rage, I vowed revenge.

BONES AND WHITE ASHES
AND DREAMS

Snow frosted the classroom window. Snow blew parallel to the white earth. The cars in the parking lot were hooded thickly with snow. The bikes in the bike rack were blotted out. Loaves of snow swelled on the ledges. On the gargoyle stone abutments, snow whitened the faces of the strange stone animals. Sealed inside, the class murmured and shifted.

The audio-visual boy, his shirt riding loose, trundled a projector into the room and threaded the film and toddled on his geeky brown shoes to the wall-switch and dimmed the light. The history teacher explained the short film was upsetting but necessary, a supplement to our lessons.

Sliding numbers, scratches, furry dark smut. Then govs of light on a dirt lane. Jeeps passing. A campsite fringed in barbed wire. A haggard, maybe insane, woman pacing on bare dirt. More women, dressed in prison stripes, as in a James Cagney or George Raft movie on TV. Their liquid dark brimming eyes. Their shockingly skinny bodies. Their flesh in curds, wrinkles sunken plates—like the webbed skin in your thumb groove. Their bone structure revealed. Yet they're alive.

A vast area of broken earth—pits, hummock—like a garbage dump. A bulldozer, the driver masked like a bandit. Heaps of bones. More masked men, pitching white skeins toward the camera. Sunken bodies, some in recognizable shapes. Limbs tumble, faces show the spoiled remains of grimaces, scowls, perhaps ghastly smiles. Folded over, spilling. Priests at the edge of the pit, silently saying something.

American soldiers, many boyish and shocked, milling in a compound. Scarecrow survivors, men this time, and a long wooden bench in a dormitory. One holding a pair of boots tied together at the laces. Another peeling an orange. Most of them hunched over. Some peering into the camera, not accusatory but stunned. Their eyes expressing, why am I here? And, maybe, why are you photographing me?

Train movement. That seductive iron gliding, inexorable and purposeful. Rails at twilight like exposed silver nerves. A fat, impassive switchman in a soft gray cap. Steam and sparks like fog in fireflies, as the train brakes.

Bald children in the makeshift dining room. Red Cross nurses with pots of soups, ladling it for the children. Slowly, slowly eating. A mournful little girl with a cup of soup. Gumming the rim of the cup. The nurse guiding her hand. Soup slowly seeping down her chin. The nurse dabbing the girls chin.

Star of David banner furling from the window. Two bearded men, as formal as chess pieces, standing on either side of the blowing banner, the breeze riffling their hair. A yoke of sunset through budding trees. More numbers, crisscrossed scratches, then annihilating light. The projector ebbing, stopping.

Outside the classroom the snow-dervishes whirled and drifted into piles, like deep white ashes. Snow ticked against the windows, insistently. In the back of the room a girl wept and blew her nose.

The teacher said nothing, and the class made no commotion or monkeyshines. It was a lesson, but an unfathomable one. The death of millions of European Jews lay beyond reason, like the actions of my family, like the white snow falling as from some cold celestial fire, like the earth itself.

In my room that night I imagined spacemen landing in spaceships as huge as the pyramids of Egypt. They might build vast concentration camps and gigantic furnaces. They might hate earthlings as an impure species. They might transport everyone to the camps and tattoo them with rayguns. They might stoke the furnaces with the human race and all the animals, too. Birds might fly above the blanketing smoke. The spacemen, now that the earth was theirs, might caw with pleasure or dance in rings or play symphonies into the sky to harry the birds higher.

I chided myself. I didn't really like science fiction. With Ruby I had started and sneezed and we watched *When Worlds Collide* and *This Island Earth* and *The Day the Earth Stood Still*. But even as we dismissed them, we kept watching; they had a childish fancy. The Nazis were as brutally odd as any science fiction villains. Maybe their hierarchy patterned their actions on science fiction models.

Eva groaned and snored down the hall. Snow feathered against the window, and the wind swept against the boards of the house. I slid my feet into the cool margin at the edge of the bed. My head had flattened and warmed the pillow, so I slipped it and fluffed it out to get a softer feel and some coolness.

In sleep I dreamt of my mother, as I often did. She was in a gymnasium, lit by shafts of light through a glass atrium roof. A man in a drab uniform, like a mailman, commanded her to tumble, to do jumping jacks, to touch her toes. "Now I want to watch you wash. Show me," he said. There was a sink next to a trampoline. "Ten demerits. Twenty demerits." Mother stood there, very still, like a child being chastised. The light spilling down was unnaturally bright, as if cast by a beacon. Black tails thrashed on the atrium ceiling, dancing in the light. The floor had a vivid blonde varnish, it wasn't at all like the ruddy floor of my high school gymnasium. "We'll have to get the boy if you refuse to wash," the man said. He wasn't threatening; he was patient and almost sorrowful.

Sometimes in dreams faces are indistinct—you recognize the people more through intuition than actual sharp appraisal, but here, in this drama, my mother's face was irradiated with suffering. It was as if all the demands and injustices of a lifetime were pelting her. Her eyes swept the big room, pleading for mercy or forgiveness or simply an end to the ordeal. The man giving orders was no longer there; he was swept from the dream.

Still, my mother's face was frantic. She spoke, "I can't find the trees. Where are the trees? I was in my room, then I was in the hall, and somebody gave me some medicine, and I kept saying 'Where's Kenny? Where'd Kenny go? Is he in the trees? Did the dagos shoot him? Did he sell the guitar?' And nobody would listen to me, nobody would tell me a thing. I was coming down the hall and I came in here and I don't know where I am. I'm in the wrong section. I don't know who you are, I don't know what you're saying to me. I don't know. I can't find the boy, I can't find the trees, I can't even get outside. You won't even let me go outside! And I feel like dying—!

And as she said "dying", my muscles knotted and I broke through layers of sleep and dreaming, and jolted awake with cramps in my calf muscles. I lay there kneading my legs and listening to the wind and trying to erase the dream. But it vibrated in my blood. Somewhere in the night, westward from Ohio, my mother might be in peril. She might be turning, thrashing, reaching for Kenny, fighting to reclaim her sense of self, as she plunged upward from her dream.

SWIMMING

My Aunt Jitka visited from Chicago, and at Eva's behest she talked to her nephew at the A&P and arranged a job for me. Bagging groceries three hours a day augmented my exercise and made me stronger. Most of my wages went to my grandmother, but I kept enough to buy a bicycle.

That summer I practiced riding in the gravel lot at the top of the hill. I wobbled and fell a few times, but quickly mastered balance and pedaling.

One Sunday I rode over the bridge—the broad septic river below—and followed the road past scrubby lots and shabby houses until it coasted down into a lush valley. I explored miles of open countryside. The trees and foliage gleamed with every shade and half-shade of green in the spectrum—melon rind-colored ferns, sun-soaked brilliant shrubbery, dusk-green pines, emerald and lime-green roadside plants, and the basic vivid green of grass.

I rode down the long tree-shaded lanes and open patches of sunny landscape, exalting in each new vista. I bought strawberries at a farmer's market and sat under a shade tree and rinsed them with my water-bottle and ate them one by one.

I passed long meadows and cornfields and farms with big red

barns set far back from the highway. Cars blasted by me, drenching me in warm air. I came into an area of rolling hills, and the uphill climb made my leg muscles knot.

I crossed a narrow suspension bridge and turned onto a dirt road. The woods were dense, twilight-dark in their depths. I pulled into a dirt cutoff. Thick weeds grew in the center of the path. I got off my bike and pushed it along, the high grass rubbing the fenders, grasshopppers popping up all around me. I panted a little, my heart pressing. When I guzzled from my water-bottle, I could smell the strawberry juice on my fingers.

Light flashed through the overlapping tapestries of leaves. Water purled, a wonderful sound. I came in view of a creek. I set my bike against a tree, and slid down the bank to the water's edge. The water sparkled, a crinkled golden light. Off the big pink-and-gray boulders in the shallow, sparks of reflected light shot. Across the creek, the woods ran uphill, dark-green and packed solid, with the crowns of the highest pines stabbing through and swaying slightly in the wind. A tributary trickled down broad slate steps into the bigger creek.

I removed my shoes and socks and dipped my feet into the cold water. I took off my shirt and pants and waded into the water. It was shockingly cold, freezing me up to my navel. It was a kind of pagan baptism, and I was determined to dip myself. I dunked my torso and head. I bobbed up, gasping. Before this I had never been immersed in more than a bathtub full of water.

I paddled around awkwardly. I kicked my feet. In fifteen minutes I learned how to swim. There was an ease to it; it was a small fear to overcome. I got out and found a shady spot to snooze.

An hour later, when I woke up, I had a painfully taut erection. I was always dismayed by this phenomenon. Masturbating would relieve the discomfort, but I couldn't do it here, exposed in the open world like a satyr's apprentice. I needed the darkness and privacy of my bedroom. I dozed again, and the descending sun aimed rays into my grassy nook and warmed my lap. Jarred awake, I felt gouts of semen springing against my creek-dampened shorts. The smell was pungent and vital, like a swap through which a clear stream fed.

I waded back into the water and rinsed my shorts in the current and rubbed the stickiness away. I felt peaceful in the eddying water, whose own wet skin had broken discs of light dancing on it. Above me, on the bank, a shade tree with odd, mossy, tawny leaves caught the sunlight. It was a solemn-looking tree, and it reminded me of the Chinese peasants in *The Good Earth*, a movie I'd watched on TV at Ruby's house. It was strange, and anti-climatic, to view locust swarms and pestilence one second, and a guy with gummy hair and psychotic eyes hawking carpet remnants the next, but that was the only way you could watch an afternoon movie on TV.

Water plugged my ears; the blood trapped inside me gonged softly. Floating on the sunlit water, I thought of birth-fountains and gushing seed, and death-fountains and spurting blood. I thought of sex, drifting beyond the tribal schoolyard smut—the fuck-jokes that all hinged on awkwardness, buffoonery, slipshod hygiene. I drifted past my earliest erotic fantasy, of a shy, mute, slender girl, like a servant girl in a fairy tale, who let me embrace her and kiss her pink lips.

I drifted past all the impediments of flesh and spirit and ego, the pubescent dreams where my clothes were shucked, as were hers, and we kissed, licked, whispered, spoke, fit into each other—I with my peg of flesh, she with her complicated pink pestle, so tender and mysterious and suddenly pen, and in the trembling aftermath of what we did, acts that were unnameable and beyond the lexicon of schoolyard obscenity, we'd make noises that weren't words but were a lovers' shared code, like birdsong in a tree at sundown.

I couldn't describe the place toward which I drifted. It was there, tantalizingly. Love. Happiness. Simple-sounding words, but so difficult to achieve. Circumstances as strong as gravity or mortality balked people, and prevented love and happiness. So the unloved and the unhappy ran rampant or lurked waiting, and they were vengeful. Wounded themselves, they'd wound others, and rub salt in those wounds. This vengeful roundelay and folly of the human race defined its history.

As I floated, I felt the perilousness of my dreams of love. An iron difficulty most likely lay ahead for me, when I was grown and gone from Ohio and searching westward for my parents, and everything else that could feed my heart. A long, harsh butting of headstrong wills might complicate my future, as I navigated into the land of the unhappy, the love-starved, the obsessively vengeful. And I feared that I might be a nomad like them, that hatefulness burned inside me and scorched the possibility of love. I could flounder like Kenny or flame out like Leos or just prowl the land in a dwindling dream of happiness, until I found a room, a blanket, a candle stub, and lay still in desolation.

To shock myself out of this reverie, I swam underwater. Twisting upward, I emerged like a merman. I had the damndest thought: had crotchety old Eva ever swam in clear water? Had she ever loved? I remembered a tumescent insomnia, a few days back, the cresting, tickling pleasure in my center, as I fondled myself. I spoke to my fantasy-lover, indistinct yet palpable in the darkness of my room. "Shhh. Keep your eyes shut." I ejaculated endlessly into the sheet, my body convulsing. As my heart decelerated, Eva shifted and groaned down the hall, and I had an annihilating hallucinatory flash of her in my bed, heavy and grumpy, and my skin was prickled by a thousand needles of revulsion. Yet I felt a sadness for Eva, alone and groaning her old lady's groans and perhaps reaching for the shape of Leos, obdurate as he was and long dead.

So death and loss and shame and revulsion could seep into us in the aftermath of love and pleasure. What a sinking, dreadful realization, that our memories and imaginations were layered so perversely, like a cathedral over a carnival over a mausoleum, all three leaking into each other without volition.

I swam toward an overhang where the roots of the mossy tree pierced the bank and floated like hair in the water. I dove down and frog-paddled toward the cave beneath the bank. The water was murkier here; clots of mud worked loose as I nudged the dangling Medusa roots. The roots suddenly multiplied—no, it was a swarm of watersnakes wriggling past me, uncoiling like small whips, some three feet long, others smaller.

Startled and afraid, I broke the surface and flailed backward. I turned my body and swam back to the far bank, where my clothes and bike were.

I rode home directly into the sunset, a maelstrom of pink clouds topped by thunderheads. The last few miles, it pelted rain. I skidded a bit on the wet asphalt, my tires singing. The trees thrashed silvery specks of light. The rain plastered my shirt to my back and made my eye-sockets sting.

Turbulence in nature was magnificent. There was no malice in it. We should all, the entire forlorn tribe of humans, let the rain cleanse us and expunge our hatefulness. Let it patter on us until the rhythm of the water convinces us that grief and vengeance will ebb like a river into a sea, and the sea will carry it away, and it will be gone forever.

THE KNIFE

In West Cleveland it was traditional, and even prudent, to own a weapon. On a cold Saturday morning I went to the Army-Navy store on Prospect Avenue and chose a knife. It was honed, wicked, expensive; it came with a leather sheath. I carried it home in my pocket. Riding the Rapid, I watched the bleak winter scenery ram past the windows—smoking-cold streets, the manhole covers leaking cold vapors; warehouses like penitentiaries, with stacks of pipe and long accordion rolls of fencing in their yards; then the factories on their miasmal plain.

I hid the knife in an old boot in my closet. Eva called, "So you gonna eat or you gonna vait?"

I went to the kitchen, where she tended her pots of stewed chicken, dumplings, paprika gravy. I quartered two apples and peeled the skin from hers; I sliced some cheese. We ate slowly and silently. Eva nibbled her apple pieces grudgingly. The table was covered in ancient cheesecloth whose red-and-white checkers had faded to water pink. I dredged a dumpling through the rusty-orange gravy. It tasted good, actually; it was Eva's company, heavy and woeful, that was the problem.

I considered prowling around that evening. I considered the satisfactions of delinquency. But I kept to my room, leafing through Orwell's *Animal Farm*. It didn't have the horror of *1984*; the satirical pigsty bickering was weightless. I browsed through my dictionary—the separate, elegant, evocative words. Maleficent, malleable, mammon. The factories, the schools, the churches, Nixon and Agnew, the music business the bewitched and betrayed my mother—they were all mammon.

The dictionary, in the most inward and undetectable way, empowered me. I absorbed the exact words to pin down the phenomena of the world. Vigilant, vinegary, virago,—there was my grandmother, if I kept my sympathy in abeyance. Self-sufficient, sensualist, sentinel—there I was, with my aloneness, yearning, watchfulness.

I knew that I could never flaunt any fancy language. My teachers expected mediocrity; they would frown on linguistic peacock antics. It was hard to resist twitting them in my school essays. I was at the age where it was always tempting to write "obsidian" where "black" would do.

I kept going in the dictionary, all the way to zygote and zymurgy, as Saturday night burned away. Cars sped by from time to time, and rowdies flung a bottle at our stoop. I would have to sweep up the shards in the morning.

In the night I dreamt an alternate, disturbing version of my visit downtown. I was back in the Army-Navy store. I felt gooseflesh on my arms—my mother was beside me. "Show us the big silver one," she said to the clerk, who was hideously old and ill-looking, not at all like the actual anonymous clerk who had taken my money that afternoon. My mother smiled, coquettishly; it was a dream gesture untrue to her nature, because she was always polite and grave with salespeople. She drew the knife delicately along her forearm; tiny rubies of blood grew from the wound.

Inside the dream I was trying to say, "Don't, don't," but I was balked, mute. Mother spoke very softly, "Let's pay up so we can go." On the counter she plunked tattered bills, all singles; and a spill of pennies and silver. I squirmed in my claustrophobic dream-space as she counted it. She didn't have enough to buy the knife. I stood in a trance. Stricken, neither my wallet nor my legs were quite there, and in fact I couldn't even reach to pat my pocket, because my arms were unhinged, inoperative. I was wrapped like a mummy in sheer physical helplessness. "I guess we'll have to go see the distributor," mother said, woozily. She began to blur. I was engulfed by dream-nausea, dream-fear.

I woke up with a dry mouth. It was near dawn, black shading to the darkest blue. I moved through the dark to the closet, and squatted under Eva's hanging clothes bag, and eased my hand into the boot. I unsheathed the knife, stroked my knuckle alongs it's edge, and re-pocketed it. Where in the wide, swallowing world was my mother? She hadn't called in nine months.

In a little while I could hear the church bells tolling in the decrepit neighborhood churches. There was a chalky-white frost on my window, and through it I could see the dry brown vines on Mrs. Syzmanski's trellis. I pinched my eyes shut and snuggled deeper into my sleep-warmed bed. Sinking toward sleep, I fixed on an image of mountains, chains of mountains, rolling westward in the pink dawn. The solemn noise of the bells was heraldic, worthy of the mountains in my mind and not the drab churches. When they stopped tolling, I was asleep again.

EROTICISM AND DANGER

In May I rode my bike far earthward, where there were estates and big parcels of unpopulated land. The trees were in bloom again, pale-green and white and rose-pink, and the rain-dampened countryside reeked sweetly of earth and flowers. Burgundy-colored blossoms blew like confetti in the breeze and flew at me as I pedaled by the softly storming, color-shredding trees.

Far out in the country, I turned down a lane of widely spaced houses, each set on acres of trim greenery and backed by forest. Sliding glass doors reflected the sunlight, and awnings shone like forged silver or aquamarine gemstones. At the end of the lane, overlooking a field of wildflowers, there was yellow ranch-style house. The garage was open, but there was no car parked there.

Without any plan, I dismounted my bike and pushed it into the field and leaned it against some sumac bushes. Dusty saffron flowers clung to my pants. I approached th house swiftly from the side, practicing a sentence in my mind: "My I have a glass of water?"

In the backyard there was a small flower garden, nasturtiums and violets and white roses, and a birdbath brimming with caught rainwater. I dipped my finger into it, stirring sediment at the bottom. I looked into the back door. I knocked and waited. When no one answered the door, I jimmied it back and forth, but it was locked. I found an open window and stood on a cedar lawnchair and pried at the screen with my fingers. I hit the screen with the heel of my hand and it collapsed inward. I boosted myself through the opening and slid backward over a sink, tipping a small glass with an avocado pit in it onto the floor.

"Breaking and entering" was a familiar term in our neighborhood. I had never thought of doing it, but now, magically, I was doing it. Perversely and thoughtlessly, people just did things. I was glad that I'd left my knife at home.

The kitchen was neat, the counters wiped, all the surfaces lit by mellow sunlight. No oppressive meat smells in the air, no brown paper bags crammed between the refrigerator and the wall, no soot in the puttied window crevices. I opened the refrigerator—juice, yogurt, milk, fruit, salad dressing, and tiny cork-stoppered bottles of serum or medicine. I sniffed one; it was powerfully bitter. I took a long swif of orange juice.

From a bowl on the table I broke a banana off the stem and peeled it and devoured it. I stuffed the peel into a trash container. I drank some water from the tap. I cleaned up the smashed glass and set the avocado pit on the sill.

Acutely aware of the squeaky-soft sound of my tennis shoes, I explored the living room. The furniture was white of lemon-colored—it soaked up the sun, and even had a faint citrus odor. On the mantel above the fireplace there was a framed picture—two teenage girls in tennis whites, their arms linked, smiling. Both had long brown hair and clear eyes, candid eyes. My heart began to knock.

I went up the hallway and found a bedroom. The room was cool and faced away from the sun. The bed was outsized and covered with a white satiny spread. I stroked the spread and peeled it back.

Underneath was a canary-yellow blanket, very soft in texture. Beneath the blanket, the sheets were creamy, silver-white, and definitely silk. I caressed them, marveling at the texture, knowing that I had experienced this sensation of silken touch before, long ago. Yellow, white. Yolk, sunlight. Egg-white, silk.

I was stunned, tranced.

I stood by the window and looked across the shadowed lawn to the sun-flooded field. My penis arched, pulsing. I shucked my clothes and shoes. I lay on the bottom sheet. I pulled the top sheet, also silk, over me. I shut my eyes and elased into an ecstatic, prone trance. Eventually I spoke names, words, sounds, to evoke the girls in the picture. "Myriam, yriad. Sarah, saraband. Waterfall, wuuuhhh." Deep inside, in another voice I heard "Joe, Joe, Joe," ringing back at me, like a conjured cry of love.

My heart pumped pure heat, as did my groin. I turned onto my stomach, lifted slightly like a lover, and slid my penis against the silk sheet, and the friction was exquisitely pleasurable. Usually, when I masturbated, I was brutally quick, as if inducing a seizure through sheet speed. Now, in this stranger's bed, I moved in gentler strokes, making love to the phantom girl. When I ejaculted finally, I left a plate-sized smear on the silk. I lay shuddering and eddying on the silk, my belly and thighs jellied with seed.

I was unable to return to myself at once, and I didn't want to. I was in the after-throes of unique criminal satisfaction. I lazed there, mindlessly, my eyes shut, my emotion shunted aside but still distantly vibrant.

I kept my eyes closed a little longer, then unlidded them so that I saw a sun-blood-red swarming rectangle. Then I came back to myself, Joe the housebreaker and bed-violator, alone and wet on this stranger's bed. Back in my old skin, I walked to the bathroom. I washed my groin and belly and thighs. I dried myself with a big white towel.

No matter what, I could never return to these luminous, private rooms. I felt a solitary, criminal sadness. I got dressed and retraced my steps to the kitchen. I ate a ripe peach and put the peachstone, with its scarlet threads and sticky orange shreds, into the trash can.

There were flies buzzing in the kitchen—I had left the screen on the floor. I set it back in its frame and tamped it tight; the metal fasteners that secured it hung loose on the frame.

I left through the back door, locking it behind me. Half the grass in the backyard was plated green-gold, the other half in soft green-gray shade; they joined together in two long triangular wedges. The birdbath was like a religious statuary, but in honor of a god worth worshipping. I still had bits of golden chaff on my pants. I felt calm and sated. I stood there for a moment, musing, on the edge of the shady triangle. When I walked across the sunny wedge, finally, the sun felt magnificent on my skin.

My god was born on the heat of the sun, and on the currents of touch and texture and ecstasy. He was a god who would permit me to glory in real flesh, to ease into it with my aching peg and stroke myself and her, her, her, to love and release.

That was the word that every living being must murmur in moments of prayer: release. Release me from the torment of my solitariness, God. It was what birdsong meant, and the lowing of beasts, and the seething, shuffling, muttering noise of people, alone inside themselves, or walking through the world.

Release me, God.

DEATH WATCH

During my senior year in high school, doctors diagnosed cancer in Eva. It festered in her stomach and bowels. She refused the operation, the cutting, the therapy. A hospital was purely terrifying and alien to her. She preferred to sit at home, taking painkillers and drinking herbal tea. Enthroned in her big chair, she grumbled and groaned and meditated on her misery, stubborn as a stunned ox. In the last few weeks of Eva's dying, my Aunt Hana came from Pittsburgh to tend her.

Hana was eight years younger than Eva, and in an early stage of feebleness herself. She had arthritis; her hands were mis-shapen and clawlike. The veins in her legs wormed to the surface of the flesh, and she walked with pain. Furrows and mottles and blotches the color of red cabbage marred her face; there were earth-colored pouches beneath her eyes. She scolded and bossed me relentlessly, but there was no force of malice in her manner; it was just part of her domestic protocol. Briskly and impersonally, she ministered to Eva, as they were old adversaries. Every morning Hana stewed prunes and apricots into a compote and fed a little to Eva, whose lips turned brown and dry and finally refused to open.

The day my grandmother died was an unusually hot one for April. The sun baked the puddles in the yard dry. It parched the sidewalks, turning the fallen blossoms into crisp brown dregs. A warm breeze stirred the linen curtain in Eva's bedroom window.

Hana sat hunched in a chair beside the bed, holding Eva's hand and lamenting the lives of the seven sisters; how they were scattered across the continent, most married unhappily, two widowed; how they begat nine children among them, all of who were scattered in turn. Hana didn't sentimentalize the history of her broken tribe; she burned the same bitter fuel of memory as Eva.

When Hana mentioned Karin, Eva's eyes, which had been flickering faintly, opened wide. She gasped and gargled and coughed and subsided. She forced out the words, "Gone after dat no-good. I tell her dat, but she...Gone to Cheah-cawgo after dat no-good."

The hatred rose in me, and I chanted silently, die, just die. When I looked at Hana, she had some pity in her eyes. It my have been self-pity or pity for the mothers of all wayward children, or pity for Eva, who burned gall even as she expired. Hana had one son, Steven; he was a navy lifer who'd come to in the brig with vomit on his shoes more than once. He sent Hana postcards, from Hawaii and Australia, with one-sentence greetings.

Late that afternoon, the priest came—not Father Kerensky, but a younger, whey-faced specimen. He constantly wiped his damp forehead; he was terribly uncomfortable in his heavy black get-up. When he spoke to Eva, her eyelids pulsed, but she didn't answer. Perhaps she was renouncing everything at the end.

Hana, who had quit the church years ago, gave the guy the buzzard-eye. I relished his squirming discomfort, and kept a cold stare on him myself. It was a wonder that anarchists didn't dynamite churches on a regular basis; Christianity, to me, was nothing but a fount of misery, superstition, and hypocrisy.

But Whey-Face was resolute; he wasn't bamboozled by the eyeballing that Hana and I gave him. With some gentleness, in a muffled plangent voice, he gave Hana the last rites. He and his blasted church forgave her everything. I couldn't forgive her, though; I blamed her, in part, for the absence of my mother.

The priest offered to stay, but Hana shooed him to the door. We sat with Eva and took turns cooling her brow with a washcloth. Hana tried to make Eva drink water, but she pursed her lips against the plastic straw, as if it were the lance of Death itself. God sat, tapping his toes and humming, as Eva died. In her dry fever, she managed a couple spasms of speech. "Not da boy. I vanted—" I must be the boy she meant; she rarely called me Joe, and never Joseph.

A few minutes later, she said, with clarity, "Elena. Vy she vent—", and that was the name of her youngest sister. Her lips palpitated, she shuddered once, and she died.

Hana patted Eva's hand. She bent over and kissed her colling cheek. I felt a stab of nausea, as the slow-motion ghoulishness of her bending hit me. Hana thumbed Eva's eyes shut. One rolled a little, showing a bit of cloudy white. Hana thumbed it again. She pulled the sheet up to Eva's neck.

I took Hana to Mrs. Syzmanski's house, where she phoned the undertaker. I led her by the elbow home; she walked with agonizing slowness. Birds were hopping on the small plot of grass in Eva's front yard. There were beige bristles, torn loose from the broom, on the porch steps. Far out over Lake Erie, beyond the factory smokestacks, an airplane pursued the last slice of orange daylight across the horizon. The evening air tasted delicious.

We both dreaded returning inside, where it was stuffy and reeked of Eva's dying. We sat on the porch steps. Hana fetched two butterscotch candies wrapped in foil from her purse, and we sat sucking them.

"So now what you gonna do, Joe? What you gonna be when you're grown up and everybody's gone?"

"I don't know. Graduate from school and leave."

"Where to?"

"Somewhere in the world." I tried to shrug, but shuddered instead, like a horse bitten by flies. In the quiet evening, outside the oppressive house that I so hated, I sat and felt the suffocation of my life. I had to leave soon, or smother to death as Eva had.

"Why don't you call Ruby?"

"Ahh, Hana. Ruby and Eva hated each other. What would be the point?"

Hana clucked bitterly. "I don't know the point, Joe...What about your mama? How's she gonna find out?"

"Please don't, Hana. I—don't—know—where—she—is." I clawed at my eyes. "She hasn't called since Christmas of '73. She was in Nevada then...Goddamn Eva to hell, she's why mother wouldn't come back."

I wanted to spit flame like a dragon, but I knew that Hana was innocent. I wept helplessly.

"That's better." Hana patted my shoulder. "Cry for Eva. We'll all cry a little."

"It's not for her."

Hana sat in silence. My anger was replaced by shame. I tried to say something soothing to Eva's soul, if it hovered near, if it hadn't been snatched up the celestial flue. But I couldn't form a eulogy or apology or panacea. Eva was likely on her own, flying toward eternity or oblivion or rebirth.

Pragmatic Hana snapped me out of my daze.

"Eva left you the house. She told me. It's worth something. You sell it—go to college, do something good."

I shook my head. I kept all images of my mother at bay, but I thought of Kenny. He might rejoice, strike a jubilant chord on his guitar, if he knew Eva was dead. I heard him say once, "When the old bag croaks, I'm gonna buy a six-pack and drive t' the cemetery and drink 'em down all the way out there, and when I get there I'm gonna take a long, satisfying piss on her grave."

BURIALS

We buried Eva in a flat, ugly cemetery surrounded by a hurricane fence. The gravestone was a modest vermillion rectangle—Eva herself fearing anonymous burial, had purchased it from a stonecutter—with her name and dates and nothing else. Five of my seven great-aunts attended the funeral—Elena stayed in Washington and Aunt Ilse had moved to West Germany. No one would cross an ocean for Eva; all but Hana dispersed that afternoon.

Until June Hana stayed in the house, acting as my guardian. It wasn't too grim; Hana had a tartness that I appreciated. We didn't cook much, leaving Eva's pots and pans in the dishrack. We ate fruit salad or rice pudding, and drank iced tea. I brewed the tea and sat it on the counter to cool, with a plate over the bowl to deflect soot.

In May I turned eighteen and in June I graduated, one of four hundred solemn students ambling across the stage of a concert hall to receive a diploma rolled in a tube and sashed with a crimson ribbon. We sold the house immediately. Hana kept Eva's silver jewelry and a few gold coins. The Salvation Army hauled the furniture away.

I gave Hana $2000. With part of my $6000 I bought a used Chevy. I rented a small trailer for the summer. It was set in a rural park, with the odors of manure and hay wafting in from nearby farms, and a mountain ash tree providing color and a willow some shade.

Driving was hazardous at first. I had passed Driver's Education and gotten my license the year before, but I was apprehensive behind the wheel, driving too slow and braking often. I was baffled by the aggressiveness and irrationality of other drivers. I stayed on country roads and drove toward the Pennsylvania border, gradually becoming accustomed to the mechanics of it.

I studied maps and plotted a course westward. I decided to search Chicago first, to look for the crumbs of my mother's trail. I was iced over with fear when I thought of her. If she had succeeded, made money, found happiness, why hadn't she called? Why hadn't she sent for me? I dwelled on scenarios of attrition, loss, catastrophe.

Like a pilot light inside me, the warmth of my mother's touch— her late-night gentleness, hovering at my pillow—fired me. Yet I could feel the light wavering, tapering, threatening to flicker out. It was an awful, familiar fear: to be slammed shut inside myself, separated forever from warm attention, loveless. So terrible a fear that it could harden from fear to resolve, attain a star-like density of lovelessness.

I squirmed and fretted in my narrow bed, cupping the heat inside me, hoarding it. No matter how ravaged or disappointed my mother might be, no matter what Kenny had done or not done, certainly I would embrace her, soothe her, as the heat flushed my fingertips, my chest, my limbs; as the water burned, inevitably, in my eyes; as everything dissolved, like sugar in hot tea.

I planned to leave in September. To burn energy, I swam daily in the small chlorinated pool that sat at the edge of the park. The lifeguard's chair was empty, but I usually had two fat, friendly ladies for company. They wore sun-hats, and their soft upper arms were reddened like lobsters and dabbed with Noxema. Drawling and clucking, they counted my laps. Their names were Loretta and Sage.

I did ninety-pound curls with my clattery barbell weights. I was five feet ten inches tall and weighed a hundred fifty pounds. I was still a virgin and I worried about my awkward sexual status and castigated myself and practiced endearments and erotic twinings in my dark trailer, with the wheezing air conditioner as a spooky reminder of Eva's nocturnal rustlings and groans—the lonely crepitation of people and things, in their separate spaces.

In early August I rode my bike twenty miles to the creek that I'd discovered two years before. When I reached the cutoff, I was dismayed to see two cars parked in the scrubby field. Pushing my bike cautiously toward the creekbank, I heard a ruckus.

Through a gap in the foliage I watched three boys, all burly, swimming. When they emerged from the water, teasing and slapping wavelets at each other, my heart jumped. I recognized Archie Pollard and Danny Trevino; the third one I didn't know, but he was a boisterous ass-slapper just like them. I retreated. I pedaled back to the trailer park, and floated in the pool until my aching muscles were eased.

The fear that I had for Trevino and Pollard had lain dormant for almost four years. At school they had shot a few jibes at me, but they had never accosted my physically since the day that Trevino raped me with the twig.

In my trailer I dug around in a box and retrieved a paperback. It was *The Painted Bird*; on the cover were two Hieronymous Bosch figures—a greenish humanoid with a hawk's beak, and on its back a pale, stunned boy, riding in a basket. The book overflowed with violation and insane cruelty—a European cruelty that seemed, nevertheless, actual and provable. In one passage, Russian soldiers sack a village, and one barbarian is so unhinged that he rapes a fallen villager anally, even as the man is dying. Reading that, I felt a ripple of pain from my breast to my anus. In history, millions had been isolated, spattered, killed; it didn't happen only in a novelist's, or painter's, fever.

Bosch and Kosinski would probably consider the cruelties of Trevino and Pollard too petty to tabulate. They were boys; and they were so nonchalant. Through high school, I watched their style change. Outwardly they ameliorated their character; both dated girls, both played on the football team, both were presentable. But I knew that they were innately cruel, that they were my enemies, that they were like Tartars waiting for a village to plunder.

I sat on the sofa that was attached on a frame to the wall of my trailer, and fulminated. The images of their water-frolic replayed in my mind. I remembered the afternoon of my violation, the soaked-red wad of cotton spiraling down the toilet bowl, the sting of the alcohol.

There were barks and yowls in the distance. Dogs were mating, or treeing a raccoon, or just blowing off energy. I turned off the lamp and lay in the dark. Sweat crept along my neck and the backs of my knees. Going asleep, I soothed myself by thinking of geography—Alaska (an icicle sound), Maine (horsehair combed by the wind), Ohio (curt yet rounded, like a well opening).

The next afternoon, I debated whether to carry my knife along. Since I feared my inflammatory hatred, I left it in the kitchen drawer with the cutlery and can openers. Along the route to the river, the roadsides were sullied by animal carcasses—raccoons and woodchucks and a black-and-white cat with its teeth in a death-sneer and its salmon-colored guts burst through its fur where a tire had crushed it.

This time, only a station wagon was parked in the turnoff. I guided my bike through the high, swishing grass. I peered past the wind-riffled leaf-cover and saw Arch Pollard, sunning himself on a big rock and smoking a cigarette.

In a trickle of stones, I slid down the bank. I skinned my ankle on a sharp wafer of rock embedded in the bankside, so I went immediately into the water and laved the torn skin; the blood slipped away, like a tiny red squid.

Pollard regarded me calmly. "Ho ho, it's Joe. How goes it Joe? Haven't seen you since graduation, boy—and you were lookin' pretty grim then. Two-hundred-and-eight cunts, one-hundred-and-ninety-two cocksman. Four hundred on the button. Pretty worthless ceremony, huh? Wudju do with your diploma, Joe—burn it? Pollard took a last puff, and launched the cigarette butt on the water.

I stood in the shallows, watching him. I backed onto the bank and pried off my wet sneakers. I took off my wet pants and set them next to my shoes. I was bare-chested, sun-browned.

"You're still mad at me, aren't ya Joe? Old Archie. The prankster. The crankster. You crank any cunts yet, Joe? Or are you holdin' out for true love? You even hold hands yet, Joe? You can tell your Uncle Arch." He splashed his feet in the water.

"Didn't anybody ever hit you in your repulsive mouth, Pollard?" He chuckled. "A couple times, yeah. But they didn't do much damage. Didn't wreck my self-esteem...Couple little ratfucks tried t' coldcok me, but I slapped 'em off..Hell, Joe, don't be a prude. You want a beer? I got some in the water here." He dangled his arm beneath the surface and fished out four beers fastened together by a plastic rim.

He tugged two loose and dropped the other two off the rock. "Here." He flipped me a can, hard; it flew at my chest, and I caught it. "Go ahead. Taste some suds. We're just a coupla puds with our suds. Say that ten times fast, Joe. Lighten the fuck up." Lazily he scratched his thigh.

I lifted the tab and depressed my thumb, and the shaken beer fizzed out and foamed over the ridge. I tasted a little; it was bitter.

"That's it. We'll have a couple beers. Then a joint. Then we'll go check out some cunt. The area's crawling with cunt, Joe. Excuse the terminology. Sorry...With women...They got us outnumbered, actually. Even when you throw out the unfuckably ugly ones, there's plenty left. Let Uncle Arch be of assistance, Joe. Let me be your cunt-guru...Whoops, there I go again...Woman-guru. I'll help break you in, Joe. I always liked you. Hell, you're my buddy. Smart... quiet. Wry little guy like you, with the big brown eyes and everything, ought to be up to his ears in women. You could score, Joe. But you gotta talk. Forget that strong-but-silent shit. That won't work, usually. C'mon. Talk to Uncle Arch. Tell me what'd feel good—slippery little blonde cooze—somethin' like that."

"I got very little to say to you, Pollard." I lobbed my beer can into the river; nearly full, it sank. In my black swimtrunks I waded toward the rock where Pollard sat. I stopped in waist-deep water, maybe four feet from his perch.

"My feelings are hurt, Joe. Joseph. What're you all pissed about—that football prank we pulled a few years ago? Must be that." He took a long swallow of beer. He slipped his can into the water and it bubbled full and sank. "Hell, I sympathized. We probably went overboard way back then. I'd be a little pissed too if I was you. But I couldn't be you, Joe. I couldn't get myself in that kind of hassle. I mix and mingle. I'm friendly."

Pollard beamed at me. "I've seen much worse shit than what happened to you. Christ, one night I saw JoAnn Lasefkowitz, 'member her? I saw her get fucked blue. Maybe twenty guys. I wasn't one of 'em, either. I'm not slidin' my ole cock around in everybody else's muck...Anyway, they just pronged old JoAnn 'til she didn't know her ass from a goalpost anymore...?"

Pollard wagged his head. "Point is, there she was in the lunch-room next Monday, eatin' an ice cream bar and grinnin'. No big deal. She didn't have t' pack herself off to a rehab clinic or any-thing. That's the trouble with you, Joe. As I see it. You're such a goddamn sulker."

My heart was ramming, but I kept my voice steady. "You're such a goddamn coward, Pollard. You stand there and watch rapes. You assist. That's your trouble. As I see it."

"Awwww. Whadda we gonna do with you, Joe? You're star-tin' t' irritate Unky Arch. It could be pointless t' talk with you, but here—let's try this...You're not interested in cunt. Okay, takes all kinds. What gets you off? A little fairy sprinkle some fairy dust on you? Way back in the cradle maybe? Is all this grudge shit just some roundabout kind of fairy approach? That's okay. I'm here t' help, Joe...See this?"

Pollard slid his shiny, royal-blue trunks down onto his thighs, displaying his flaccid penis.

"There it is, Joe. Get him goin' and he's a real throat-choker. That's what all this is about, isn't it? You been pinin', all through school and everything. You wanta suck the old salt-hose, get your tonsils painted white. Okay, sure. Will that settle things so we can be buddies?"

Pollard stroked his penis. He smiled. Without any clear plan or thought, just purely infuriated, I waded up to the rock and yanked his leg and spilled him into the river. He outweighed me by at least fifty pounds, but I was strong—and stronger yet, at a pitch or mur-derous rage. We were in chest-high water, clawing at each other. I caught his neck in one hand, digging my nails in. His flesh was thick yet pliant, like rubber. I pulled him under the water, using my other hand to press his buoyant head down when it burst the skin of the river.

When he thrashed out of my hold and came up a second time, Pollard choked water. I hit him with my right fist, but I missed his nose. His cheekbone felt like iron. I turned in the water and elbowed him in the nose, which crumpled. He let a whinny of outrage, "Goddamn fucker!"

He boosted himself out of the water and onto me, wrestling my torso in a clumsy underwater dance, since we were both shoulder-high in the river now. He managed to topple me underwater. I floated parallel to the surface, like a mummy, peering up in panic at this hovering bulk and the broken, sun-dappled water. I kicked outward and surfaced a few feet downstream. I heaved sour gouts of water that strepped my throut and burned my nostrils.

I bobbed up and down, the water to my chin. The sky was blue and blazing; a few ghostly wisps of cloud floated eastward toward Pennsylvania. Pollard scrambled into the shallows and bent over and tugged loose a large rock and hefted it. Dark silt ran down his wrist; the rock had a muddy undercoating where it had been socketed in the riverbed.

Pollard waded toward me.

I swam a few strokes into deeper water, my heart thudding. Where the bottom plunged from four feet to six feet deep, Pollard slipped. I moved toward him as he snorted water. He couldn't swim properly and carry the rock at the same time. As he bobbed and began to lift his arms, I drove my elbow again into his face. His teeth split the tough meat on the point of my elbow. He made a slobbering, smashed sound. I seized his hand in which the rock was fitted, still dribbling muck, and pried it loose. With both my hands I drove the rock into the center of Pollar's face.

Roiling the water, Pollard sank. When he rose up, his face was featureless and bloody. He gurgled, but couldn't yell. Blubbering and in shock, he sank again. I let the rock slip from my hand and it grazed my leg and then my foot as it settled on the creekbed. Beneath the water I saw Pollard's ballooning blue trunks, lodged on his thick thighs, and red swirls like ink flowing from his burst face.

I swam ten feet and crawled out of the water and sat on the bank, panting, my heart and lungs seared. I drank the warm air for half a minute, making decelerated gasps. If anyone had arrived to interrogate me, I couldn't have given a single coherent answer.

On the far bank of the creek, near the downhill-flowing tributary, Pollard clambered out of the water. He sprawled on a rock slab. I dove back into the creek and swam easily across and came out below him. He held his hands over his oozing, ruined face.

I climbed the shallow shelves of rock, wary of slipping. The rocks were sealskin-gray, with slimy moss in patches and uneven encrustations that made my feet lurch. I stood next to Pollard; I was his conqueror, yet I felt sickened rather than triumphant. He dropped his hands. In the bloody mess of his face, his eyes were distinct—one vivid brown and canny, the other bloodshot and partially eclipsed by swelling.

He tried to talk. "You hit me for? You fuckin' shit. You hit me for?" His voice was pleading, aggrieved, reduced to a rasp by the battering and the swallowed river water. He embraced me around the knees and my feet slid on the slippery rock. I keeled on top of him. His mouth—with is bloody, coppery odor—snapped at my face. I felt his tooth in my lip. I used all my strength to jam him backward, and in wrenching around he must've broken his leg, because it made a loud popping sound. He bellowed in agony.

I didn't care. Hatred flooded me again. In both hands I graspd Pollard's hair, not too long but still a substantial curly mop, and drove his head into the slimy gray slab, where a crayfish scuttled away and small pebbles shot like alkaline bubbles across the shallow, sun-brightened water. I beat Pollard's head into the submerged rock until the water clouded with blood and he quit struggling.

I lay back on the clammy slab and shut my sun-blood eyes and sobbed silently. In the field toward the road, mourning doves cried liquidly. I sat upright, then stood. I ached all over, fiercely.

I grabbed Pollard's ankles and bumped him down two levels of rock and dragged his limp body into the creek. His blue trunks were snagged on his knees; his genitals and buttocks were fish-white. Blood leaked from the quicks of my fingernails, where I'd gouged and grappled with them. I had cuts and abrasions from my wrist up to my shoulder. My lip leaked a red syrup, which sucked back like a vampire.

I waded into the creek, pulling Pollard like a raft behind me. His head submerged and bobbed back. I towed him along against the gentle current toward the overhanging tree roots, where the creek was deepest.

Pollard's body sagged, floating heavily. I unleashed it. I took a deep breath, preparing to dive. Pollard's head tilted toward the sky and he rolled over, reaching his fee toward the bottom, and gasped. He spat water and pieces of bloody inner cheek, or tongue.

I was nearly exhausted, but I dove and swam around him and snatched his leg. It must've been his injured leg, because when I flipped above the surface, yanking him askew and underwater, he shrieked until the water filled his shrieking mouth. I got his other, wriggling, kicking leg, and held him like a wishbone, head down toward the bottom.

I held him like that for maybe two minutes, then let his legs go. I dove under water. Small tinctures of blood spread from his face; stirred silt muddied the water near the bottom. Still buoyant, Pollard began to rise. He thudded weightlessly off my arm. I rose with him, holding him like a barrel.

I swallowed air, cradling Pollard's limp neck. Faintly, he began to gasp for air. My heart engorged, I went under, rolling Pollard and pressing him beneath me. We sank like Siamese twins into the muck of the bottom. Under the floating tree roots, I maneuvered him into a small cave-like space. When I wedged him, he sat partially upright, his head butting the tree roots, his hair oozing and waving; dark earth, loosened from the roots, muddied his face.

I sprang to the surface, my lungs pumping toward explosion. I swam to the far shore. I sat on the lowest level of gray rock and held my face in my hands and wept drily, as Pollard had minutes or hours ago, and tried to fathom what had happened.

I had been an attacker, then a defender, then a murderer. Once we'd started battling, there had been no time to puzzle out the logistics of a standoff or a treaty or an apology. In combat we were no longer reasonable or human. My throat ached terribly; I might've screamed in rage or terror or victory many times during the battle.

I was in an inhuman bind, and there was nothing to do but to continue. I spent the next several hours gathering rocks, stones, broken tablets of shale. I ferried them across to the overhang, a couple at a time, and descended with them and piled them into the cave, on and around Pollard's sagging corpse. I entombed Pollard in rocks.

Too exhausted to go back to my bike and unclasp my water-bottle, I drank directly from the swirled creek. I might've swallowed the merest tincture of Pollard's blood, aswirl on the current.

I steeled myself to leave. On a dry brown hummock of grass, I found Pollard's sun-baked clothes and his canvas shoes holding his wallet, keys, cigarettes and lighter. I retrieved my own clothes and staggered back to my bike. Easing my bike along, the two sets of clothes draped over the handlebars, I walked slowly to the road.

Pollard's station wagon sat frying in the sun. When I touched the door-handle, it felt as hot as forged metal. I dismantled my bike and put the frame and wheels in the folded-down back seat. I peeled my trunks off, wrung them out, and looped them over the bike frame. I put on my clothes and shoes; it felt microscopically comforting, not to be nearly naked and visibly bleeding and wet as an aquatic gladiator.

In trying to rev the car, I flooded the engine. I sat sweating on the plastic seat cover. There was a toy warlock fastened to the center of the dashboard, and a squashed milkshake container on the rubber mat. I turned the ignition key and the engine fired, pinging like my heart.

I drove eastward, the fiery sun sinking behind me. I whizzed past two bicyclists; one had thick, muscular legs like Pollard, and I glanced into the rear view mirror to make sure that the cyclist's face wasn't bashed and oozing gore.

It was nearly dusk when I pulled into a shopping plaza and parked opposite a patisserie shop that was closed. I wiped the steering wheel and door-handles with Pollard's shirt, a burnt-orange cotton pullover with a yellow yachting insigna stitched on the tit.

I reassembled my bike, shielding myself with the open door. Next to the patisserie was a leather good shop, and from its doorway an old man with a shock of frizzy white hair, like the actor Sam Jaffe in *The Asphalt Jungle*, emerged. Behind him toddled a child dressed in a cowboy suit, with chaps and toy guns in holsters. The man painstakingly locked the door, grasped the child's hand, and led him slowly and gently up the sidewalk toward the mall concourse, from which a few straggling shoppers issued.

I tied both sets of clothes in a ball and crammed it into the basket attached to my bike. I rode twenty-five miles southeast. Behind me, at the western horizon, the sky was like the slit in a kiln, brick-red. When it got dark, I kept to the berm, ticking gravel into the ditches, wincing as headlights raked me occasionally. When I arrived at the trailer park, I felt exactly like a bone-weary, bludgeoned, raggedly cut and scraped killer. Which was what I was, inescapably.

A STONE INSIDE ME

For several days I sat inside my trailer with the segmented glass window blinds shut and the air conditioner laboring. The cuts on my face were like sutures; a marbly pink scab—like the sparkling river rock that Pollard sat on in the sun—grew on my elbow; my bit lip swelled; my eyelid went from plum-colored to a greenish-yellow; my gashed legs burned and itched as they healed; my fingertips throbbed, and a crescent of split skin beneath one nail stung fiercely for days; my head pounded ceaselessly, as I worried, agonized, felt pangs of guilt, re-ran the murder in my brain. I took aspirin in abundance, and they soured my guts, because I couldn't eat.

Worst of all, I remembered details. That, when I first went ferociously face to face with Pollard, I could smell his smoky cigarette-breath; it had the pyre-like harshness of my grandmother Ruby's mouth, up close. That, when I jammed Pollard into his muddy grave, small air bubbles dribbled from his torn mouth—that he was alive yet, and choking water, and begging wordlessly to rise into the warm afternoon air. That, as I plunged upward, my launching

96

foot kicked him, and he tottered sideways into the cloudy brown muck, like a statue settling into the cavebed. That, in the car, his shirt smelled vividly of cologne—he might've worn it the night before on a date; its lime scent tickled my nostrils in memory.

I had an absolute fear of reading a newspaper; of seeing the story of disappearance; of feeling my heart jackhammer; of knowing that only I had the solution to the mystery. To picture the cops, prowling stone-faced around the station wagon, probing its upholstery, was to feel absolute animal fear, and helplessness. Would they track down Pollard's three-hundred-ninety-nine classmates and grill them all? Would they coast to a stop outside my trailer and climb wearily out of their cruiser and knock on the metal door, before my cuts healed, before I could rehearse some plausible lies?

If I were to resume my life, I would have to erase Pollard. I would have to let him fray and dissolve, alone, in his stone-and-mud tomb, with only the eerie, graceful watersnakes slithering around him. I went to sleep with images of the river playing like a movie in my mind, and I often dreamt scraps of water-dreams, borne along on the noise of the pumping air conditioner and the distant hissing of cars, as strange and invasive as whale songs. I burst awake near dawn with the river jiggling in my consciousness. It was like a water-command barked at me: Start here, monster. Every day. Remember the thrashing creekwater, the bleeding face, the rocks.

In a week, it faded imperceptibly. In ten days, it shrank a little more. I recuperated. I began to feel marginally sane, passably human, mobile enough to drive to a restaurant and eat a hamburger steak and a baked potato and a large salad.

The food was delicious, sacramental. Sparrows sat in the tree beyond the plateglass window. The waitress was a shy, pretty ash-blonde, awkward in her squeaky loafers, who brought me more pats of butter for my basket of bread and more ice-water, delicious too, in the sort of amber plastic tumbler that restaurants stock to prevent breakage. You couldn't break one of those tumblers with a mallet.

I went home and packed, grateful for the mercy of diminished awareness; grateful for my few possessions and my ability to flee, for in America you could slide like mercury on glass, and grateful for the heat in my heart, that sustained me even as it had plunged me into turmoil, that beat and beat and blasted my memory and gave me volition to go out into the word, scary as it was.

Pollard lingered, but farther down, like a scar that ached when the weather changed. I prayed for his soul, if he had a soul. I prayed not to God, whom I distrusted as a trickster and an absconder, but to myself. I prayed for tranquility and forgiveness and love. I prayed to be released, permanently, from the rage that had seized me at the river.

I walked out in the darkness to the ashy-smelling trash barrel and burned Pollard's clothes and wallet and stirred the scarlet-and-gray ashes with a twig and let the twig fall into the barrel to smolder, too. I left my bicycle outside my trailer for some kid to scavenge. On my last night in my little gunmetal-gray trailer with its groaning, wheezing, grandmotherly appliances, and its green-tinted bottleglass window blinds, I vetoed my arrogant atheism, temporarily, and launched my prayers toward God Himself, in his cold celestial bed, just on the odd chance that He existed. Something might exist out there.

I prayed to find my mother, alive. And I kept going—I challenged God, like a donkey braying at a mountain. Out of the depths of my romantic and sexual voraciousness, I prayed to find a woman who'd speak to me and let me enter her and rider her flesh with all the love that I could muster, until I was exhausted, oblivious, and floating serenely in a place beyond murder and isolation, because I could never survive there, no, if I was trapped there, I would dissolve in the mud of my prison, like Pollard in his underwater crevice, and it would be worse than death, that must subsume peace—it would be a grinding hell that turned the blood on my heart to ichor; and I would be not Joseph Telezynska, a human being, but a monster, who took his revenge, as a monster must, in hatred and revilement and murder; and I would stampede through the malign world, seeking Trevino and slaying him, and slaying all the rest, too—anyone who'd ever dominated or betrayed me; I would be a beast.

I fell asleep praying and woke much later, deep in the night. I was sweating and trembling. I could only remember the last bit of my dream; it wasn't a water dream, but odder. I was walking in a botanical garden with my mother and Kenny. Yet they didn't acknowledge me, didn't touch me. Kenny fed a guitar pic to a big sunset-colored parrot, as my mother scolded him. Kenny began to caw, and his face expanded and contracted and broke apart in chunks, like a hallucination. There was a blurry stretch—probably I was trying to struggle awake, and thus causing the dream-images to rack in and out of focus. Then Kenny's face was whole and proportional again, and he capered like an illusionist who's tricked an audience, and he said, "That's how to eat the old bird." Vibrating in my head as I lurched awake was the dream-reaction of my mother, aghast, looking at Kenny, who was so casual in his ghoulish wizardry.

I never understood my father, never had a chance to question him about his motives, his behavior, what lay in his heart beyond the need for food, shelter, status, a little love. That he would do something inscrutable and say something nonsensical, in his dream-incarnation, seemed apt. I was coated in gooseflesh, and I knew that I wouldn't be able to return to sleep.

I packed my few plates and kitchen utensils and my sheathed knife. In a shoebox I had a dozen photos of my mother and my diploma and a copy of her family tree that Hana had given me. I had a carton of paperback novels and my two dictionaries and a tiny blue leather keepsake of Eva's, a wedding souvenir that was no bigger than a passport, where the guests were listed and the date of the wedding inscribed, March 27, 1936. Eva was thirty-two when she married, thirty-six when she gave birth to my mother, seventy-three when she died.

I left the trailer key on the sinkboard. I put my gear on the back seat of my copper-colored Chevy, because the trunk had rusted through and was untrustworthy. The upholstery spouted wadding and the dashboard had a moldy rime and the steering mechanism was erratic, pulling to the right. But I loved the car as much as I could love a machine. I felt easeful inside it.

Beads of copper-colored dew glistened on the hood. I swished the windshield clear of dew, yet thin streams continued to angle down it. I pulled onto the foggy road and drove through the dark countryside. I felt hypnotically attached to my long headlight beam; it annihilated the dark.

I zoomed onto the freeway and, in sparse pre-dawn traffic, soon traversed the lit skyscrapers of Cleveland, topped by the spire of the Terminal Tower and beautified on the outskirts by a cathedral that blazed in a pimento-red aura, like an architectural heart.

Westward along the blue-black lakeshore I sped toward Chicago.

2

SCENES FROM THE BROKEN TRIBES

HAROLD—CLEVELAND—1980

The sign on the door weaves its letters through wooden birds carrying branches in their beaks: HAROLD & BESSIE POLLARD. The lawn is thick and green, the tulips and lilacs in bloom. There is a bed of pale-orange nasturtiums by the backdoor. Against the siding of the house a baseball bat, its tip dank and rotted, leans.

Harold sits in the recreation room in the basement in an old red leather chair with bronze studs along its throne-like back. It's thirty years old, but the leather still has a sheen. The basement is a warehouse for their castoff furniture now. Too sad to give it away, though some day they will. The Ping-Pong table has a plastic shroud, and Bessie has parked two lamps on it.

Harold sips scotch. He's taken his tie off, but he's left his work shirt on. It has a plastic pen-holder in the pocket and a spot of creosote on the sleeve and stale pits. He wears his gray work-slacks. He's barefoot, enjoying the cool stone against his hot, tired feet. He'll change later. Bessie's gone to play bridge and won't be home till after ten.

Harold turns on the old basement TV to the baseball game, but can't recognize the players. It's a team of transients. He turns it off ten minutes later. Archie had his collection of Cleveland jokes, and the Indians were always a favorite target. Anecdotes of ineptitude were told and retold—outfielders colliding to allow a slapstick inside-the-park homerun, pitchers balking with the bases loaded and two out in the ninth. Archie had an ecumenical love for baseball. He latched onto underdogs, simultaneously bemoaning and appreciating their worfulness.

Harold pours more scotch. The name keeps rapping away in his mind, obstinate as a woodpecker. Archie. It never goes away. Never.

Harold is past the point where he can form words and sentences or codify his grief at all. It isn't even permitted to be as final as grief. It's a clot of shapeless misery that will likely be inside him until he dies or transforms or goes crazy. Tentatively religious once, Harold has left the church. He finds tiny grains of pride and resistance in forsaking God. It gnaws him that there can be no reunion with Archie, no fusion of souls. But Harold accepts, pridefully, that his own soul is lost.

Bessie is the spiritual supplicant, the hopeful one. She's managed to keep her faith and, blessedly, has not resented Harold's disavowal. Sharing the suffering has helped them survive. Now Bessie has her bridge outings twice a week, and her choir practice. Indeed, her contralto is the only force that could lead Harold into a church ever again. Shyly, he sat in a pew on Easter Sunday and listened to the massed voices sing Schubert.

Bessie has her volunteer work, three afternoons a week, at the Animal Protective League. Her two dogs, Ripple and Tennessee, road the spacious fenced-in backyard smelling the grass of their domain, trotting back and forth, chewing and burying their bones. Harold tries to love the dogs and can't, quite.

He can't stop thinking. Not words but images. Archie's car, a white station wagon with dented fenders and a Cleveland Browns decal, sitting its space on the big asphalt lake of the parking lot. Lit by flashbulbs, aswarm with men with tape measures and fingerprint kits. Tweezing the floor, filling plastic bags. Sand, grit, pebbles, some blood that wasn't Archie's.

Harold circles back to the most terrible memory. It's etched in his own guileless words. Months after Archie's vanishing, he and Bessie lay arm in arm in the dark, like inexperienced lovers, and the thoughts formed and Harold spoke without pausing to weigh the words, "If Archie had been female, maybe they would've kept her alive. Sometimes they do, killers. Even if it's just to torment her some more. Or rape her...But maybe she has a chance that way. She has a little chance...Archie was so strong, he would've fought. There had to be more than one of them, Bessie. Archie would've fought and fought. There's no way, Bessie. No way..." They wept together for a long time but it didn't help, nor could they embrace with any ease in the hot, mussed, inescapable space of their marriage bed.

Nearly two years have passed, and it fades only a little. They sleep together but never make love. Harold is fifty-five, Bessie fifty-one, and they still feel some sexual heat and a palpable love. Yet it must stay stoppered inside themselves. They never discuss it, don't have to. Two weeks after Archie was reported missing, Harold caressed Bessie at the waist, absently and she covered his hand and lifted it gently away and slid six inches toward the wall and continued to grasp Harold's hand, letting him feel that her skin was still warm, yet showing him too, that the space must be kept. And he accepted the silent decree, gratefully even, because how could he ever make love to his wife, when every motion and meaning of the act would be suffused with grief? He couldn't.

Harold has his prospering hardware business, and now a small adjacent lumberyard that's doing well. The smell of wood is like a memory from a happier life, hammering a doghouse together for Archie's collie. There's always plenty to occupy his mind at work. If only he didn't have the evenings to suffer...

Having just one child is risking big sorrow. He knows that.

All the money bet on one number. It can break you when it doesn't come up. Now Harold has another image that bedevils him: a cemetary on a clement day, a few people in suits, some wreaths and flowers. If only they could find Archie's body—just the bones would do—so that he could be buried...

Harold lets the thought snap. He finishes his scotch. He goes upstairs and turns on the oven to warm his supper. He continues out the back door. The dogs dash to him in the twilight to be petted and to slobber on his pants.

In the darkness he goes back inside and turns on a couple lamps. He lights the porch to guide Bessie's car in. He eats a few bites of meat and potato, and takes the rest outside for the dogs. Too many table scraps are fattening them. Tennessee has the equivalent of a potgut. Harold knows that he should walk them more, but he always pictures himself as a mournful man strolling in the dusk, all the neighbors spying from their porches and nodding sadly. He can't do it. He has to stay on his own property in the evening. Some nights he putters in the garden, while the dogs come up behind him and nudge him with their damp noses.

He stays upstair after supper. It's like a small test of strength— don't go back downstairs, don't brood. The bright fabrics that Bessie likes don't have the proper effect. They're like festive lights at the border between happiness and despair. They taunt somehow. His heart won't allow him to criticize Bessie. In truth, dark fabrics would be no better. Yet the flowered chair-covers, the yellow-and-orange quilt on the couch, the framed samplers on the wall, the comic birthday card propped on the end table—they all feel wrong. He keeps the lamplight low when Bessie's gone.

Harold pours another scotch from the decanter. He tries to read *Sports Illustrated*, but the sentences snag. The infernal collegiate brightness of the article gallshim. He puts the magazine down, dims the light, and just sits.

Bessie shows up at quarter to eleven. She changes into her robe and Harold joins her to shed his work ensemble at last. He puts on his own robe. They sit in the living room and have a drink together. Bessie's bridge club has a preponderance of teetotalers, and she needs the warm scotch afterwards. As they sit on the couch in the evening coolness, verdant smells coming in on the breeze, Bessie spreads the quilt over her legs for warmth.

At her urging Harold lets the dogs in. They scramble around the room, threatening to tip tables. Ripple gets his heavy front end up in Bessie's lap and licks her face. It takes the dogs a few minutes to settle down. Harold gives them biscuits and they sprawl on the rug and crunch them. Tennessee growls a little when Ripple moves his snout toward some loose biscuit crumbs. They are both mixed collie/golden retrievers, brothers.

Harold switches off the lamp, and there's just the soft glow from the light above the kitchen sink. A foot apart on the couch, they sit in the intimate near-dark. The dogs are both dreaming, twitching, their metal dogtags jangling against the floor. Bessie makes her characteristic cooing nose in her throat. Fondness, empathy, and an urge to merge with all the forces of life—all expressed in that miniscule throaty coo.

Harold has an impulse to shout, but it's not ungovernable. It passes like a flash of heat. Instead of shouting, really, he wants to reach across the foot of space separating them and squeeze Bessie's hand. But he knows that a squeeze can be misinterpreted. It can feel like a spasm of hopelessness. He doesn't dare touch her, doesn't dare touch anyone. Bessie coos, very softly, once more.

EVA — CLEVELAND — 1977

The boy leads her to bed. Her short, heavy legs are wobbly, and the pain in her center upsets her balance. Her cane mashes into the floor so that the boards squeak. She knows that the boy, Joe, hates to be near her. When he holds her lightly by the elbow, it's not gentleness — it's fastidiousness. Easing her onto the bed, his hand glides over her calf, and his fingers pull away as if seared. He speaks one word only, "There."

She sinks into the sheet and immediately grows hot; a polar death would be so much more merciful than this burning cancer. Joe returns with water, ice cubes clinking in the pitcher. He pours her a glass and helps her drink, tilting the glass. She can hear him breathing. She settles her head, her dirty mass of hair, onto the pillow; she will ask Hana to shampoo her hair in a basin — she doesn't dare ask the boy.

As she shuts her eyes, the boy reaches in with a towel to dry her chin. The heat inside her intensifies, and the pain is like an elements of the heat. Her heart thuds, and she feels a spreading weakness.

Joe leaves, his steps quick on the old floorboards. She drowses and groans softly and thinks that she hears a mouse in the wall. Mice could come and nibble her like marzipan and she wouldn't care. It's even funny; she manages a gnarled laugh, imagining the mice nibbling her candy ears, her broad candy nose.

She lulled. She sleeps a little, and as she sleeps islands of time break loose inside her and slide into the ocean of memory. Every time she's able to sleep in these last few days on earth, she drifts in the dramy sea-wash of memory—

In 1922 she left the village, thirty miles from Brno. She rode a ways with Menzel, a Moravian poultry farmer. She carried a pasteboard suitcase and a knotted black-silk handkerchief that contained bills and coins and two flawed diamonds. Her five remaining sisters waved, skipping along the cart track. Next to a beech tree her mother stood and watched, less ceremoniously, shading her eyes as the cart clattered away.

They traveled past Brno, where the mills puffed out a great stench, and under lowering skies clattered northward across the plain. Menzel had crates of chickens, laying hens and cantankerous roosters both, that squawked and shat and flapped up and down against the crate-sides incessantly. Dogs darted out of the roadside scrub and ran alongside, spooking the fowl.

Early autumn rains soaked the fields. The earth was brittle brown, then a tawny mud, then chocolate-dark and nearly impassable in low places. Sodden campfires along the road reeked on lignite and wet coal. Enterprising peasants roasted potatoes in these fires, where they could shield them in a kind of lean-to, and sold them to travelers. Eva chewed the mealy, tasteless chunks that nevertheless warmed and filled her, and one night Menzel chose a noisy hen and beheaded her and plucked her and chopped her and put her in a stewpot so that they could have chicken soup.

Her kidneys and back ached from the jostling of the cart.

Menzel made little effort at conversation—mostly he complained about the dispositions and antics of the chickens—and the journey was far more tedious than adventurous. Weeks from Brno, they passed through a wet forest in the morning mist and saw red-hatted soldiers ahead.

Near the Polish border Menzel sold his fowl and hired another wagon to take Eva to the Baltic and embarkation for America. The negotiations were secretive, subtle—Menzel had to do considerable wheedling to obtain Eva's passage. He left for Brno with his chicken money and a big black turkey, tied by its hind leg to a chunk of broken axle, the bird wouldn't fit in a crate.

The Polish family that gave Eva a ride consisted of an argumentative husband, a browbeaten wife, two mewling girls, and a pensive little boy. They rode for long, rainy days, skirting Lublin and then Lodz. Eva huddled under a cloth tarpaulin, musky straw prickling her legs and thighs. The narrow clay road had deep, peeling ruts that brimmed with yellowish muck.

She snuggled against the girls, who whimpered in the night. The husband and wife took turns at the reins, not stopping till after dusk. Their horse had raw wounds where the wet harness chafed. Despite the lack of a common language, Eva grew tender toward the boy. She hoisted him up so that he could urinate off the side of the cart in the slanting rain. When they arrived in Gdansk, she kissed all three children goodbye, for even the temperamental girls had grown happier under Eva's care.

The cargo ship permitted twenty-four passengers in steerage, four each in six cramped suites. There were no beds, just horsehair pallets. Communally, they used a massive chamberpot; twice a day, one of the men carried it to the deck and jettisoned its contents overboard. The voyage was a test of the nose and the stomach. Besides the open chamberpot, they could smell the grease on the pipes and, from the cargo hold adjacent, a rank chemical stench.

They ate saltfish in oil, hard bread, potato soup, figs. When Eva's digestion revolted, she climbed to the deck for air.

The sky was darkening above a wide opalescent whirl of brightness. Her eyes smarted at the treacherous radiance. She watched the horizon flush pale-yellow and gradually blaze down to a few red rays, like a stirred fire. Darkness snuffed the sky shut and rolling clouds blocked the starlight. The ship's lights spilled running at reflections on the black water. The cleaving motion of the ship soothed Eva. The meaning of the word ocean was revealed to her as benign.

The other passengers were a goulash of Poles, Germans, Magyars. Some of them were acrimonious, and fought like blood enemies. Eva was shy, abashed—unable to mediate the fights. Suitemates were shuffled in order to avoid outright murder, and she ended up with three Polish sisters.

In Halifax harbor blocks of ice floated, and gulls swooped and shrieked in the cold air. They berthed at a dock with a big, three-sided warehouse attached. It was open to the sea, and stevedores stood waiting and clobbering their hands together to fight the chill. As they unloaded the reeking cargo, young boys in dirty chapeaux and suspenders and high boots circled the bales and whacked at escaping rats with clubs.

The next morning, the ship followed the Atlantic coast southward. It was slate-gray and chilly when they docked in New York. Jitka met Eva in a vast dockside shed. There were flags and bunting and pennants with snakes and stars with kettle drums, furled from the rafters. Alien voices echoed in the huge space, hectoring American voices. When they embraced, Eva was mortified because she hadn't had a proper bath in two months; the odor of the voyage clung to her. She would never forget soaping her armpits with harsh gray soap over a basin of cold water, as the three bulky Poles spied and hooted in Polish.

They took a bus across Pennsylvania. The big red-and-white machine, and the paved roads, were wondrous to Eva. Beyond the cities there were autumnal forests, harvested fields, dark-green pastures. Rolling farmland in the soft violet twilight. Horses frisking and promenading far out in a field. Barns with iconographic markings. Rock cliffs and lamplit shacks in the hills outside Pittsburgh. A lantern-lit carriage pulled by Percherons. A child in a pale-blue bonnet holding a pumpkin.

Eva watched it all whisk by wanting to grab at things that stabbed her curiosity, but also afraid. The inexorable speed of the bus was frightening. What if an ox crossed the road, or a line of children holding hands? She was afraid to ask Jitka about the possibility of vehicular catastrophe. Blase Jitka leaned across the aisle in a confab with a lady in a black dress, both speaking broken crabby English.

In a panorama of dawn sky and high buildings Cleveland sprang up. Along the shoreline a gang of men in white trousers and jackets, as strange and spectral as ghosts, was spindling trash and detritus with trident-like implements. Eva had been too numb and tired to apprehend new York City—she had slept, her head on Jitka's lap, as they rode through the deep canyons and took the highway westward. And she'd dozed in the Pittsburg terminal, as the bus huffed and shook in its graphite-smelling berth. But now she was alert and eager, studying the vivid orange clouds and necklaces of cars shimmering cityward. Yet her heart stirred with fear, too; she could be a tiny dry pea, lost in a huge canister, swallowed up by the city.

Eva learned English grudgingly. Jitka coached her in food terms, sexual slang, street directions; and, much later, in refinements and niceties that Eva couldn't master. For twelve years Eva lived in the same rooming house—she knew the varnished scroll of the stair-rail and the crimson cabbage roses in the wallpaper as intimately as her own flesh. To make money, she sewed and mended. Her younger sisters—Zdenka, Hana, Elena—all made the ocean voyage. All passed through Cleveland, but none stayed.

Eva earned her citizenship in 1927, but her fear of America, of the world, never dissipated. Perhaps her sisters shunned her when they saw the circumstances of her life—her little room overlooking a bare courtyard, her meager possessions, her lack of romantic prospects. She wasn't an exemplar of American bounty and adaptation.

Their coolness hurt and bewildered Eva. Washing and feeding and playing with her sisters—these were the keystone intimacies of her life, the memories that kept her heart from shriveling. Now, in America, they all seemed politely dismissive. When Eva tried to give Hana fifteen dollars, Hana refused. She said—in the makeshift English that she had learned, so soon—"You need it more, dear" And there was no fondness in that "dear". Eva felt herself as the outcast, the yokel, the stumpy little spinster who shaved her legs twice a year.

Jitka married a plumber and moved to Chicago in 1930, where they prospered. She sent Hana postcards with pictures of museums and opera houses, and these illustrations of culture, success, assimilation, pricked her. What could she send in return? Black-and-white candid photos of urchins diving into the Cuyahoga, or Wroclaw the streetsweeper scraping horse dung into his metal scoop?

Gaunt and harsh, Hana still managed to find a husband in Pittsburgh, a meek Polish brewer name Eil, who followed her capricious commands always. Nada and her husband tended a small hotel in Los Angeles. Elenda, the beauty, married an orchard keeper in Washington. She, too, sent beautiful cards—of Puget Sound, of oceanside mountains capped in snow and shredded cloud like angel's breath.

Desperately, Eva began to attend the Friday night dances in the neighborhood. Polka bands played; the musicians dressed in a garish corruption of European folk tradition, nothing at all like the fiddlers in ruffled white shirts and the farmboy flutists she recalled from her girlhood. Eva danced with awkwardness. She drank cider and listened to the murmured assessments of the other women. They would guess covertly at the size of a man's penis, temper, bank account—"The cock, the character, the collateral," one vixenish blonde snorted.

For months Eva waited. Without saying it or even thinking it, she knew that she would accept a widower, a scarface, a reformed miscreant, a wanderer with Spanish or Italian blood, anyone as desperate as herself.

Leos attended many dances before he asked Eva to dance. He drank beer, and ducked into a back parlor to roll craps. He danced gracelessly, and this was a relief to Eva. His speech was herky-jerky and critical, but he was courtly in a blunt way. For weeks he wooed Eva on the sly, on the periphery of the dance floor.

Eva mistook his attentiveness for protectiveness, and she was both alarmed and flattered when Leos slugged a drunken older man who'd asked her to dance in too offhand a manner to suit Leos. When she went out on the terrace with Leos, he shrugged off the scuffle. "I kill him next time, maybe." In his rough hands he cupped Eva's face. His kisses tasted of ale and tobacco. She accepted the taste of him.

Leos was derisive of marriage, yet he offered to marry her a month later. "We mess it up, we mess it up—so what?" They took a bus to Buffalo and spent their honeymoon at Niagara Falls. Watching the booming, vehement falls, Eva stood five feet from the rail. Drunk yet agile, Leos straddled the rail and craned his head out and saw the crashing water merge with the upside-down sky.

Add fire to the mix, and it could be a flashback to the creation of the universe.

In the years of their marriage Eva quit trying to puzzle out Leos's character, his outbursts, his beer-sodden depression. He was stoical and embittered; he wouldn't discuss his history beyond a few heroic details of fights, skirmishes, bets won.

Katrinka was Eva's only hope in the world. A soft-faced happy blonde baby. Every moment of washing, dressing, feeding, tending her daughter gave Eva a sense of soulful absorption. These tasks, these motions, these tiny wrigglings of the fingers and brushing caresses, these movements in sleep in the crib—it's all I need. As a young girl, off to elementary school, Katrinka was loving and responsive. She and Eva formed a tacit alliance against Leos. Eva protected the girl, always, from his tantrums. And, to be fair, he loved the girl in his gruff way—dandling her, croaking a song, taking her to the zoo to see the monkeys and bears.

When Leos was bludgeoned to death, Eva's grief was balked. She had the house, Leos's pension and death benefits, and her own savings. She wanted to see Katrinka flower, nothing else but that. But the girl did poorly in junior high. Quarrels erupted. Eva had no pliability, no modulation—helplessly, she lurched from total love to punitiveness. She smacked Katrinka, cursed her, begged her to behave—and Katrinka spited her.

When she was fifteen, Katrinka ran away. Hana and her husband Emil came from Pittsburgh. It took them two days to track Katrinka down. As Eva protested, they bought Katrinka dresses and sweaters, they bought her a ukulele, they took her to a Cinerama movie. But nothing could mollify her or reconcile her with Eva. She flaunted her bruises to Hana, and called her mother a witch.

They battled without quarter. Eva began to dread Katrinka's coming home, and she accepted defeat bitterly. Katrinka stayed out all night on her sixteenth birthday. She quit school the next week.

She defiantly shortened and Americanized her name to Karin.

At nineteen she had a child with Kenny, and she moved into Ruby's house. Ruby worked as a truck dispatcher then, and her consort, or common law husband, Luther, was a part-time machinist and full-time lowlife. In Ruby's yard, shorn of grass, there were goats, rubber tires, a junked Nash, stolen lawn furniture, flattened cans, beer bottles—

Eva wakes from her long dream and takes a pill and gulps some cool water. The pain in her center weighs tons; she's an elephant of pain. Hana is due the next day—despite their differences, Eva must accept her aid. Toward nightfall Joe brings her soup. He helps her to the bathroom, and she feels her urine as molten—

When Karin ran off to Chicago, Eva tried to love the boy. But he was as unyielding as his mother, and at a much earlier age. Sometimes his words had a cold precision and arrogance that lanced her. Eva recalled Karin holding and rocking and whispering to Joe, and the boy's rapt delight, but he didn't like to be held by her. She couldn't find an entrance to his world, so she shrank back.

He often spurned her cooking. From the first grade on, he dressed himself. At the slightest sign of a disagreement, he clammed up and refused to acknowledge her argument. In frustration she shook him, slapped him. Her heartbeat drumming in her ear, hating herself as she lifted the strap, she beat him—a few times.

When he was twelve and strong enough to resist, Joe said, "Never touch me again. Not in any way. I mean it." her skin felt frosted. She felt pain in her heart, in her womb. Much later, she blamed her cancer on her family hatefulness—attrition in the guts.

She let Joe be, left him alone. With Karin gone, she had nothing left in the world except her daily meals, her sewing, her memories. In memory, desperately, she even began to idealize Leos.

It could've been worse. In many ways Joe was a good boy. He earned excellent grades, was never delinquent, did his chores without complaint, took a job at the A&P and gave her a share of his wages. He read books. He knew every scientific term. He could describe the surface of the moon, of Mars, of the stars. He could talk with Jitka and Hana fluidly, when they visited.

Eva internalized her sorrow. Disappointment was the ground bass of her life—Leos, Karein and Joe were the strands of melody. She hated the dirge-like sound of it, but couldn't replace it with happier music. Now, dying, memories of Karin—her Katrinka— cut like needles stitching across her heart—

Hana comes into the room, inventories everything, puts her hand on Eva's hot arm. Hana's face is harrowed. She strokes Eva's cheek, still smooth and plump. Hana kisses her harshly.

"So it's bad, huhnnn?"

"Bad," Eva croaks. She's said nothing to Joe for days, and her voice is rusty. She reaches for Hana's skinny shoulderblade.

"Where's the boy at? Where's Joe?"

"At work, I t'ink."

"You have to go potty? I take you , dear."

Eva sleeps for awhile. When she wakens, Hana wipes her lips with a cool washcloth. She feeds her warm stewed fruit, cloyingly sweet. Eva's throat is too clotted and hot to swallow more heat; a burning trickle jams in her throat, making her cough. Joseph stands in the doorway watching.

"Feed me some snow," Eva says.

The following days are all part of the heat consuming her. Eva dreams of her outer flesh on fire, as her insides are. She remembers instances of awful pain—a scalded hand; a wrenched back; Leos twisting her shoulder out of its socket once; giving birth to Katrinka—but none can compare to this slow, hot dying, the pain ebbing and blossoming capriciously. In the past she always returned to her body—the pain was localized and temporary. But now it envelops her heart and stomach and bowels. It coats her throat like a chimney flue. It waters her eyes. It burns and flares and subsides and burns again like a stoked fire. Her hair might burn like a dry torch.

That night, Eva gives up on the idea of sleep. She asks forgiveness for hitting Katrinka, for hitting Joseph, for not grieving properly when Leos died, for living her life in a long, dying, crazily self-willed fall. She renounces her lusterless imprisonment, maintained from birth to death. Not in words, but in spasms of feeling rising from the pool of heat inside herself, she affirms her girlhood dreams—the luminous places she would go, the children she would mother, the apotheosis she would reach.

Back to Moravia, back to the hut. She'd crawl back, a foot at a time, if the world would allow it. I'm here. She knows that's where she is, in this familiar bed that's imbued with the odors of her decay. The bed is already a coffin.

The horror of living in the real world, that's what she's suffered for forty-five years in America. America is the real world, Moravia the dream. How could she succumb to such a fate? She doesn't know, she can't even pose the question in her ragged English.

It's near the end. She's let Katrinka slip away. Her mind veers to Elena—the youngest sister, the only one of the tribe with golden-blonde hair, the one who looked the most like Katrinka. She can see a few scenes: Elena trotting in the lane outside their hut; Elena chasing a piglet with a stick and giggling; Elena licking the frosting on her Christmas cake. This, too: Elena squirms in rapture when Eva tickles her; her skin smells sweet.

But in her last visit to Ohio, forty years ago, Elena sat politely drinking tea and revealed very little of her life in Washington. She spoke with the driest courtesy, asking for two lumps of sugar. Her eyes were a faraway blue.

Elena drove a roadster with sideboards and a luggage rack. She gave Eva a crate of winesap apples. Eva walked her out to the curb to say farewell. Flooded by emotion, she leaned through the window to kiss Elena and said, "You're da youngest, da dumpling."

Elena patted her arm, gently dismissive, and said, "Goodbye, Eva." It had an absolute, soft finality. She drove down the hill in the morning sunlight, the red roadster shining like an apple itself. Why did Elena disdain her so?—

Hana clutches Eva's hand. The vein in Eva's wrist pulses painfully. Her temples pound—the heat has reached her head. Past Hana, who's hovering over her, she sees Joe staring at her, in pity or horror or revulsion. He flinches. Eva's heart convulses. She tries to embrace Hana, speak, cry, protest, float free, but nothing works. Her body doesn't work anymore.

KENNY—HUNTSVILLE—1976

Waiting for Selvy to return to the cellblock, Kenny has the habitual night sweats—the crying of the body for relief, fulfillment, blackout. His cell is the last on in the quadrant and abuts the thick outer wall.

Kenny's grateful when Littlefield, stumpin along on his short legs, comes to distract him. Littlefield stands at the edge of the cell, poised like a malign troll. His stringy black beard and multiple tattoos, of Amazons battling dragons and each other, are both comical and sickening. Kenny never gets used to looking at him. Littlefield's three feet six inches tall—and a Murder One peacock from top to bottom.

"Hey, Little," Kenny says. Casually, wearily. You never greet an inmate with more than cursory enthusiasm; it could be misconstrued as a love-overture or a sarcastic threat or some stray, unwarranted craziness. Even craziness has a protocol, a pecking order, here.

"That shit with the radio again," Littlefield says, canting his shoulder. "Ev'y night, that shit." In Littlefield's cell there are two bunks and a cot. His cellmates squabble constantly, one preferring country music, the other rock.

"They should compromise. Play R&B like smart people do." Littlefield titters. "We be in heah at all, if we could compr'mise? Tha's some dumb shit there, Kenneth."

"Yeah." Wearily, agreeably. "I'm a dumb shit—is right. You got me pegged, Little."

"Yeahhh. I got all you mumbletypeg bastards." He sniffs the air. "Rain comin'." Littlefield's raspy voice is rough and masculine, yet cracks into a feminine register unpredictably. "You got a dollah?" On this request, he sounds like a flirtatious belle.

"Yeah." Kenny knows that he'll have to fork it over. Nine years into a life sentence for puncturing a fry cook's face fifty times with a knife, Littlefield has seniority, and a kind of blessedness. The trustees give him things, unbidden; the most influential inmates defer to him.

Kenny takes out a bill and creases it into a paper shingle and hands it to the monkeyish little con.

"Oh-kay. Man mus' ramble now." Littlefield struts up the cell block, comically quick on his stump legs.

Lights go out at nine o'clock, and it's eight-thirty now. When Selvy scuttles into the cell, his skin is ashen; the pits in his face, old acne craters, are slick with sweat. He's very excited.

"This'll cost us, but we'll work it out later. Cold as a fuckin' igloo, too." He fans his shirt-tails and lifts a translucent frozen package away from his belly. It's six inches by three inches.

"Let's melt it down," Kenny says.

"Nah. I like the suspense." Selvy takes a plastic bowl from the shelf. He spills the letters and matchbooks from it onto his blanket. He wipes it out with the sleeve of his shirt. He splits the top of the ice-pack and squeezes the colorless cake into the bowl.

Kenny takes four small containers of grapefruit juice from his shelf, peels the foils tabs, and with quaking wrists upends them one by one over the puck. It melts with glacial slowness. Impatient, Kenny gouges at it with the handle of his toothbrush. Selvy uses his toothbrush to help. The chip it down to half-size chuckling and cursing quietly.

"Here comes that dogdick," Donaldson says from the next cell. Selvy places the bowl on the shelf. Both men climb into their bunks. The guard pauses and looks in.

"You glue-sniffers. I smell somethin' in there. I might shake this crib down, see what shakes loose." His lips shape a slow smile. "Bye now. I be back." He starts back up the corridor. It's quarter to nine.

Selvy retrieves the bowl. As the cake softens, they begin to use their fingers. They pinch pieces loose. Kenny licks frozen gin. Selvy holds the last few frozen ounces in his palm and pulps it. It squishes in slushy shreds through his fingers into the bowl. He and Kenny laugh and snuffle like rooting pigs. Selvy dips the first cocktails out.

The gin and bittersweet juice fill Kenny with instant euphoria. His head pounds with happiness.

"This'll cost us a nut," Selvy says. He hands Kenny a capsule. It has red-and-yellow-and-black specks on it.

"Oh mama." Kenny trembles slightly. He washes the pill down. The second drink calms them both. They whisper back and forth convivially, like school kids gossiping.

The lights go out in the cell. Selvy holds the bowl between his knees. The pneumatic slam of the bars reverberates. There's cursing up and down the block, a ritual nocturnal defiance. Kenny can't remember hearing the "Lights Out" announcement on the P.A.

"Let me pour," Kenny says. The small ceiling lights in the

corridor help them adjust to the dimness. The only place to get true darkness in the prison is to sit in solitary.

"You'll fuck it up. I can hear your ribs rattlin'. Besides, you can't pour it. Gotta dip that mama up, just so." Selvy chortles.

"Do it even, man. Be fair."

"Man, if life was fair I'd be fuckin' a playmate right this minute. I wouldn't be dippin' this piss-sauce with you. So just take what I give you and shut up."

Kenny doesn't bother arguing. He's never won an argument in the slammer. The third drink mixes well with the pill. Kenny floats in the radiant blended vapors. He savors the fourth, last drink. Adrift in it is a chunk of frozen gin to suck when the liquid's gone, so the last is the most potent of the four.

"Seven months and I'm gone," Selvy says. It's the beginning of his usual lights-out litany. "Easy seven. Then I'm in heaven— cause I get t' do Brenda. I'm comin' home, you little fuckface bitch. I'm gonna do you and I'm gonna do your dog if you got one. I'm gonna pound your face in, girl. Then I'm gonna tie a bag over the mess and put a collar on you and tie you to the bed and fuck you like a Chinese hooker. No back sass at all."

Kenny gets sick of this. "Oh man. Then you're back at fuckin' square one. Listen up. I been up that trail. No matter how many times you hit 'em, they don't remain hit." Kenny snuffles. "She's liable t' go buy a gun."

"That's weak. I like you, Kenny, but you're a weak little sap. How you gonna live if you let some bitch do you like that?" Selvy rattles his ice cube in his cup.

Kenny lets out some air. "Listen up. You got the wrong fuckin' woman is all. Drop her. Swap her for a coon dog. Curse her up, down and sideways. But don't go after her, man. You'll never get satisfaction." He laughs a snuffling, explosive laugh, and Selvy chimes in with a sympathetic snort. "Like the song says. You'll never get satisfaction."

"I'll get somethin', though. Have to."

"Pay attention here. Listen up. When Karin fucked me over, I felt just as abused as you do. I spent a good two years hatin' her. It knocked me for a loop, how she did me. I lost my professional standing—.

Selvy dissolves in a gust of clogged laughter.

"Yeah, laugh—you fucker. But here's the thing. Listen up. I used to fantasize about catching up with her and holding her down and using a belt on her, making her re-...What's the fuckin' word? Re-..."

"Re-enlist." Selvy laughs, mucus shredding in his throat.

"Selvy, you never read a vocabulary book in your life. You fuckin' stupid-ass hog. Re... Recant. Make her recant. Pay me back my thousand bucks and apologize and recant. That's all I wanted t' hear. That other shit, with the belt 'n' all, that won't help. I'm no sadist. Hell, I'm a thief, at the perfect worst. But I ain't no fuckin sadist. Never even had the desire for that shit, really. Except t' string my mother-in-law up 'n' blowtorch her a little."

Again they share choppy, muffled laughter—a wavelet from the dark sea of laughter. Kenny's stomach muscles hurt, it's all so funny.

Well, Karin...She's gone and buried now, Nada. Kenny swalls saliva. "I was over in the Houston jail at the time. This guard brings me a telegram from the state of California. He's all smiles—he's read it. I was the only next of kin she listed on her medical forms. Her idea of a joke, I guess. They never traced her back to Ohio. Her police record 'n' shit was all west of the Mississippi. Christ, Selvy, my boy'd be in high school. My mom sees him from time to time. At least you don't have that t' worry about. You ain't got no kids. Karin, hell...she hated her fuckin' mother worse than I did, and that's who my boy's stuck with."

"You write him or'd you weasel out?"

"I weaseled out. I was gonna tell my mom, but she's a hard one too. She might cut off my money. She liked Karin."

"Yeah. Well. At least you got payback on your woman. Maybe the medical students got some use out of her, too."

There's a pause. There's a click in the back of Kenny's throat. "Don't be that cold, man. I can't handle that much coldness."

"Yeah," Selvy drawls. "That is pretty sonofabitchin' cold. Know what, though? I'm still gonna do that cunt Brenda. You can't tell me different. Your shit don't equate with my shit. Jesus Christ and his combined apostles couldn't stop me from doin' her...She took my clothes, she took my records, she took my stereo equipment. She sold my boat, she sold my shotguns. She probably wiped her ass on my high school diploma."

"What the fuck you need a diploma for in your line of work?" They laugh helplessly.

It's not the paper value, man. It's the indig-" Selvy laughs, shaking the bunk. "It's the fuckin' indignity."

"Piles up, don't it?" Kenny says.

"Speakin' a-which—see Boles tomorrow. This shebang was on your credit card."

Boles knows I can't pay it till my mom sends moe some money."

"That may be, but it dudn't matter. You gonna have t' pay up tomorrow."

Kenny says nothing. The hard, flat pillow is getting hot. Sweat is starting to seep down his armpits. He sleeps on top of the covers always, not needing any extra warmth. Tonight, on the edge of sleep, he pictures Karin.

She's on the stage of a small Rush Street club, in her red dress and white high heels, clutching the mic stand, singing with strong but splintered emotion, her eyes shut as in pain or unbearable pleasure, blond hair loose—a white girl reaching for the blues that are just beyond her grasp, as the realization of all our dreams seems to be.

He feels now as he did then—protected in a warm alcohol-haze. It's just Karin, singing. A gust of fear breaks through the haze. His ribcage starts to quiver, his heart to thump. The protective haze was temporary then and it's temporary now. Everything's temporary. The night will pass, the warm sensation will fade, and tomorrow will be here.

KARIN—SAN DIEGO—1974

Doctors and attendants call the street Dysfunction Alley. It's a cul-de-sac with three buildings—the psychiatric ward that extends in a gallery from the ochre-colored Charity Hospital; a methadone clinic; and a blood bank where donors queue up five days a week, as early as eight in the morning. Peering through the chicken-wire mesh, Karin watches them file in when the doors are opened at nine o'clock.

All morning long, she prowls the long central corridor of the crowded asylum. She is one of the herd—smoking, shaking, arguing, filibustering. She doesn't speak, doesn't feel that she can make humane contact with anyone. She avoids eye contact. Her brain is either too empty or too full—she can't tell, when she tries to think purposefully, if the heaviness she detects is the weight of the empty container or the weight of the irrevocably shaken contents. Something is wrong.

Nurses break up a spat. Karin paces past the two fighting women; it's a dispute over a dropped bobbypin. Noises compete for her attention—patients muttering, distant muted chimes, feet scraping linoleum, television patter—but her own non-stop inner beseeching prevails. She rides on the tide of her own rant.

There's a cloying odor, and a nurse urges a patient away by the elbow. Karin keeps passing a gaunt man, stalled in the middle of the corridor traffic, smiling lewdly, an olive-drab blanket draped over his shoulder. Her heels ache, especially, from walking on the hard floors. But she keeps pacing, up and down the corridor, until lunchtime.

After lunch—indeterminate meat-paste on white bread, a little mouthwash cup of potato chip bits, half a canned peach in warm syrup—the patients with ground privileges are allowed to walk in the courtyard and sit at the picnic tables that are bolted onto the concrete. Karin has come some distance to achieve this privilege: throttled in the therapy room for fighting; stupefied by tranquilizers for weeks; made to fellate a bald, impassive male nurse; practicing a simulation of calm; carefully talking to her doctor, a half hour session every two weeks; forcing herself to eat the food—the meat patties with beige gravy, the canned peas, the mushy-cold refrigerated bananas.

Today is her first day outside in four months. Sunlight shines on the facade of the high main hospital building. Gulls swoop into the sun-shot canyon and glide back up and away, finding no crumbs. Wedges of grass and a few dandelions grow where the concrete's split. Karin can smell the ocean, faintly. Her heart slams and slams and slams.

From her purse—where patients are permitted to carry a comb, some tissues, gum—she takes the wadded nurse's blouse, the cap and the name-tag, all of which she's flinched from a locker when the dazed, blown male nurse was recovering from his ecstasy. As Karin puts the blouse on, casually, the episode kicks back at her— she can see the male nurse's brown pumpkin head, his peppery eyelashes, his squinty black eyes; she can hear his voice, gravelly, "We'll do this again sometime real soon. That was a good suck."

The distraction of memory is helpful. She clips the name-tag on. She stalks to the door—wait! She's not wearing stockings! They'll notice!—and re-enters the enclosed corridor that leads to the main hospital. At the locked door there is a plate of heavy tin, bashed and crinkled as if rhinos had charged it, and a chicken-mesh window. She hits the buzzer, and a somnolent guard on the other side buzzes back. She pushes through the door.

Striding along a maze of corridors, Karin feels electricity—a heartsick tingling. There seems to be a greater volume of air here, and it's intoxicating. The light is different, softer. The air is ripe with new smells, too—iodine, tropical flowers, fruit juice, liniment. The backs of her knees tremble. Don't faint. She passes a bank of elevators. She expects one to disgorge clambering attendants with straight jackets, wet towels, razor straps, but it doesn't. She goes across the vaulted lobby and through the electronically triggered sliding doors and across the parking lot and through a gap in the hedge to the sidewalk. Down the trunk of a palm tree a fat gray-brown animal scurries—she thinks it's a cat, or even a puppy, but she notices the stem-like tail and realizes it's a rat.

She stuffs the hat and blouse in a trash can. In her short-sleeved turquoise jersey and white short skirt, she walks downhill toward the harbor. It's euphoric to roll a mint on her dry tongue and feel the breeze wash across her bare legs. She phrases some comfortable nonsense, out of the hospital and onto the street, to grandmother's house we go. It soothes her, but underneath the nonsense lies the mean truth: both the hospital and the street are insupportable options, and she can never go back to grandmother's house. She never even met her Czech grandmother; in imagination, the woman is as foreign as Queen Victoria or Catherine the Great.

No, Karin knows that she can't go anywhere. Her life is

charred, spiked, done. She has her blood, her heart, her tired flesh, her feverish thoughts—but who could she visit these on? There's no haven.

She passes taverns and pawnshops, a poolhall with windows so smeared that the players within are indecipherable shapes, a marquee on a mosque-like theater—AIR COOLED BLACK CAESAR HELL UP IN HARLEM SLAUGHTER BIG RIP. A girl with a huge crest of pink-and-blonde hair clanks along on wedgies. She pivots and leers at Karin, like an old enemy renewing war. The random hatred of the street—Karin's never steeled herself to it, has never become a defensive hater herself.

Near the bus terminal white sailor hats float above the sunbombed surfaces of cars. Karin enters the terminal and goes immediately to a water fountain. She lets the water gush toward her heart, a thin stream trickling into a volcano. She looks around and spits the familiar dazed and uprooted travelers. Alone in the middle of one long bench, a little girl sits and kicks her legs and talks to herself. Karin feels a pang—the girl is like an inmate in a child's asylum, unraveling words that no one listens to.

There are sailors in uniform everywhere, idling arrogantly. Jug ears, crewcuts, acne like embedded red backshot. Adult rudeness, boyish shyness. Always the possibility of exploratory cruelty. Women are like lab mice to some of these guys. Karin nibbles her lip, studying the white uniforms.

She keeps her mind at a low, disquieting hum. Actual words or definite images might make her collapse, flail, dissolve on the floor. Just do it. Just do it.

She saunters along a row of pinball machines. A tall sailor eating a candy bar looms up and says, "How bouta bite, skinny Minnie?"

Karin is unsure of her voice, but she speaks, "No thanks, honey. I'm kinda in a hurry here. I gotta get my stuff out of hock." She's sickened by the poisonous ease of language.

"How much stuff?"

"A lot...A big handsome guy like you, you might have forty bucks you could spare. How's about it?"

Candyboy removes his cap and rubs his bristly head. "Is this a whore kind of a thing?"

"Look, sweetheart. I need forty bucks—bad. If that's the word that excites you, fine. I'll be a whore."

Candyboy's companion, levering a metal ball through a flashing prison, snaps, "Let's come to the lady's aid, Leonard. That's what we do in this man's navy. Whadda ya gonna do, hold out for some fifteen dollar Filipino ginch?"

"Shut up." He regards Karin, solemnly. "So where 're we s'posed t' go?"

"Okay. You want the best blowjob you ever had for forty bucks?"

"Wait up," the shorter, stockier sailor says, abandoning his pinball game. "Me 'n' Leonard, we stick together. Do us both for twenty."

Karin's insides are shifting. Unbidden sensations scrape her genitals. For an instant she tumbles through time. She's sitting in her mother's house, she's suckling Joe, it's raining outside, sheets of blue rain, his tiny mouth takes her nipple and the pinch of his gums shoots pain to her womb, her stitches pull, she looks up from the pink baby, her mother stands in the doorway and frowns at her. It's no more than a throbbing second of memory.

"Twenty a piece, it's gotta be. Follow me."

They go single file past a row of vending machines and a cyclotron of tourist attractions—sailboats and zoo animals. Opposite a wall of gray lockers, there's a bank of old-fashioned, accordion-door phone booths.

"Short Stuff, put the twenty in your hand and get in the booth with me."

Candyboy bitches, "How come he's first?"

"Because I say so. Get in, pal." With a belligerent shrug, he backs in. Karin stoops and duck-walks between his spread knees and takes the palm-dampened twenty and puts it in her purse and sets her purse on the floor. "Shut the door." She undoes the buttons on his white trousers and finds his penis, curled sideways, hardening. She kneads it. She says, "Slide your butt to the edge of the seat and hunch down a little." She shuts her eyes and sucks him; sucks him as if he were the taproot of every wrong, destructive, doomed action in her life; sucks him forcefully—until he douses the roof of her mouth with seed and gasps something that she can't understand and doesn't want to understand.

"Don't hit my head climbing out." She flinches and involuntarily licks her lips. When she smooths her hair, she feels the pulse in her temple. She feels the pure planetary weight compressing her skull. Now she has access to a little hatred. She has a flash of Kenny, in jail, down on his knees, sucking another prisoner. See what it feels like.

"This ain't exactly Romeo and Juliet, Leonard," Short Stuff says. He puts his hands in his pockets, standing next to the booth.

"She ain't tasted my big spicy jamola, that's why. First the snack, then the meal. That's why she took you first."

With dumb grace Candyboy leapfrogs in slow motion backwards onto the hard seat and slips Karin a bill and watches intently as she unbuttons his fly and lifts his stiff organ out and dazedly begins to suck it. He grabs a shock of her hair and hefts it, tugging it slightly away from her scalp.

"Faster. You said you were the best in the west and I ain't payin' for no deep-sea blow job."

Karin's breastbone presses the rim of the seat. The muscles in her legs know as she crouches on the balls of her feet. She tilts forward, her hands holding the sailor's torso. Her heart is hooked

131

and torn and pulling loose. She puts more and more pressure in her lips; licks and laves and almost chews him; wills his blocked semen to burst and drench her mouth. He sits still, his hands on her shoulders—groaning, stymied. Then he buttoms himself and leapfrogs over her.

Karin stands up, facing the back of the booth. When she turns around, she sees a family, or traveling party, of ten people. They are buying apples and sandwiches and soda from the vending machines. They have a heap of worn luggage, cardboard boxes tied with twine, serapes and hat boxes and hills of loose clothing, shopping bags topped with toasters and hair dryers, a popcorn popper the color of a flaring orange nova, a chihuahua in a carrying case. They talk, jauntily, in Spanish. Short Stuff says, "Sure was fun, ho. Don't go wastin' that forty on dope."

Candyboy says, "Work on your technique before you go braggin' next time. That was more like a ten dollar lipjob."

The sailors stroll back toward the terminal, joshing each other and throwing light jabs. Karin waits a minute or two, watching the Chicano family in a flux of eating, jawboning, possession-shuffling. The old lady, the matriarch, squats and feeds a piece of sandwich to the pop-eyed chihuahua. Karin walks past them and across the wide floor and out the door into the cannonading sunlight. Scintillas bounce of the red and yellow and hot-white cars.

A few blocks away, she finds a small park. She sits on a bench beneath a palm tree until dusk, watching the breeze break the silver sheets of water in the fountain.

She walks to a liquor store and comes out with a pint of bourbon in a bag. She picks a hotel, a six-story upright box with pigeons edging along the tubing of its unlit sign—HOTEL TORRANCE. The night clerk is the prototype of all night clerks, a study in apathy and bad skin tone.

Rimless specs cut trenches in the slopes of his nose. When Karin puts a twenty on the counter, he says nothing.

"One night. As quiet a room as you got please."

"That'll be eighteen-fifty. And if you're planning to entertain you'll have t' talk to Ralph. He's next door in the bar. Big guy in a Panama hat. You see him first, get your peddler's license renewed."

"Jesus Christ. Just give me the key. You're mistaken about me, I just wanna sleep."

"My mistake, little lady." He makes her fill out a card. When he passes the key to her, his cool, plump, pale hand touches hers disagreeably. Karen understands, at that moment, the rage of passion-killers and blowout psychos, their need to dent and rip and bloody and obliterate the offending flesh of their enemies, their urge to spatter lead into everyone and everything, and die themselves in a hail of lead.

She leaves the lobby, bypassing the narrow elevator, and climbs the stairs to room 307. She'll have to let someone else plug the night clerk. The most she could do to annoy him was to sign her full, exotic, mellifluous name on the registration card: Katrinka Isadora Telezynska.

The walls of the little room are an oysterish off-white, the bedspread cloudy-white. There are three cigarette burns, spaced diagonally at the top and bottom and horizontally at the margin, like an incomplete tic-tac-toe game. In the trough of the spread there are small woolen nubs. The spread looks luxurious, compared to the thin olive-green blanket on her hospital bed, but it has a rough, plastic texture when she feels it.

For a long while Karin sits and looks at the painting above the bed—a lifeboat between two upswept ocean waves. The boat's lone occupant expresses distress in the muscles of his bare back, as he rows. The ocean is gray-green, the sky silver-blue, the rower's trousers a strange orchideous pale-lavender. He wears a big foreign-looking hat, like a sombrero.

She drinks some bourbon and it scalds through the clot in her throat. She downs another raw double-shot to burn the jism into her belly. Little sailor babies, she taunts herself. She'd drink liquid hellfire if it would erase the last decade of her life. She's at the stage of misery where even the most unhappy youthful memories, just sitting on her bed as a teenager and humming, seem utopian.

The air conditioner doesn't work. She pries open the stiff window, jimmying it from its puttied membrane. The sounds of the evening come in, a tide of distant and near noise. Birds and beasts and humans and machines explore the evening terrain. She can make out the harbor lights and feel the pulse of the far, dark ocean. Its black cape at night is as big and dark as an idea. Perhaps someone dreamed the ocean once and it materialized and remained, always flowing in at the edge of consciousness. Inland dreamers must've imagined something else—a mountain or a snow flurry or a strange man standing in a barn with a pitchfork in his hand.

Karin sits in the dark and feels the familiar attrition of time and circumstance—love thwarted; geography scrambled; drinks, pills, needles, anything to change the temperature of the experience; so many units of jagged recall. Rocketing through the Nevada desert at eight miles an hour, two unknown men inside her in tandem, cutting her asunder with their cocks, the driver glancing back at them and telling and yahooing and using his free hand to wave an outsized cigarette lighter, making the flame lead and holding the car on the highway all the way to Reno. Jail—she never forgets the graphic smell of sweat-soiled flesh, a cheesy female smell; curses spat into her face; every blood-divided faction battling and gouging like gladiators; stopping to staunch wounds and then surging at each other again, as the matrons whooped in the corridor like pro wrestling fans; the volleying hatred, "Rip the hair out of her cunt." Hosed down in an Illinois state hospital once, flogged with wet towels, beaten till her ears bled when she threatened to tattle.

It all jams inside her, unflushable—the sewage of ten years on the run.

Karin stacks two pillows and rests her head. She shuffles through her nocturnal deck of pleasures—the names and faces of friends recalled; Kenny at his gentlest; small kindnesses; violations not forced; a cat rolling in a sunbeam on a rug in an apartment high in the sky above the Pacific coast; the perfect stillness attained once in an orchard, deep in the night, when her lips were numb from the pills and wine, yet she stood watching the moon through the trees and thought, I'm so numb, so tired, but look at the moon, I can still tell how beautiful it is.

Kenny's in jail in Texas, the last she heard. Joe's fourteen, and stuck in Cleveland. She can't bear to imagine his life. Sometimes she can diffuse her own pain, but her feelings for Joe are purely sorrowful. Her shame is unexpungable.

What could she say to Joe? Or to anyone? That, years ago, she wanted three things: to love Kenny, and to feel some small current of love, or just wayward approval, in return; to sing, and as she sang to release the emotion inside her through her voice; to make enough money to have Joe with them, away from the drab hegemony of her mother and her unhappy Cleveland history. That none of the three wishes was granted, that her yearnings were throttled. That Kenny shrank instead of grew. That her voice was raw but small, that the emotion bled downward like water through rock, into the cave inside her. That she could be crucified by feeling but not sing it out. That not even the most receptive listener could feel more than a twinge. That, eventually, club managers and booking agents, when Kenny wasn't there to shepherd her, would expect her to kneel and take their urine-scented dicks in her mouth, in order to sing two songs, or three songs, that night. That, eventually, even when Kenny went with her, he accepted it—her sexual slavery. That he would sit at the bar and nurse a beer, as she unzipped the man's pants in his office, thirty feet away. That she went westward, to Nevada, to California, back to Nevada, to California again, and waitressed, danced, stripped, hostessed, danced some more, lay on her back, knelt, lay with other women like herself on a mattress in a cockfighting ring while men in suits watched and called out suggestions, endearments, revilements. That she wanted to obliterate herself, slowly, then rapidly, with every form of narcotic she could obtain. That the suppliers of the means of obliteration made her their pet monkey, loaned her out, coached her and coaxed her and consumed her down to the nub, until she found herself butting a padded panel in a hospital ward in San Diego. That, as a nub and not a human being, not Karin anymore in any recognizable sense, she drifted for days, weeks, months, buzzed on medication, gradually accumulating a few shreds of will, sweet-talking an attendant, sprawling on a utility room floor to be penetrated, winning her outdoor privilege, stealing the things she needed to flee.

No, she could never tabulate it or explain it or expiate it. There's nothing to do but to act. Act.

Karin's tipsy as she walks to the bathroom. She skins off her clothes in the gelid light and sits and pees. She stands under the shower and the hot water pelts her and runs down her ribs. She gargles until her throat aches. She turns the water off. She sinks to the tiles—formerly white, now tartered, with the pits of mold in the corners of the stall. The tile floor is warm at least.

She finishes the bourbon. She slams the glass against the wet tile. The base of the glass stays attached to one long sharp splinter. Good enough. A cutter.

Karin curls into herself for warmth. She boosts herself up and cranks the hot water on again. She warms herself in the hot, drilling spray. She shuts it off and sits back down on the steamy floor, and as she settles glass pricks her thigh. A trill of blood seeps out and clouds the pooled water. There's hair on the drain, blocking the drainage.

Karin sits in an inch of warm water and turns her wrist and regards the bulging vein and grinds the glass shard into it. Blood rushes uphill into her palm and downhill toward her elbow. In her bloody hand she holds the glass and plunges it into her other wrist and grinds it. There.

She butts softly against the wall and tries not to sob. She waits and waits, her eyes shut. The pain in her arms branches into her guts. She feels intense nausea, as blood pours onto her stomach and legs. Karin, Karin, Karin. It's battering her to the end, her chosen name.

Send it out. Send it out like a radio signal through the void. Send it to the far rim of the universe. Send it over the rim and let it keep going.

DEBTORS

The bright snow, falling mysteriously from the sunlit sky, made the driver want to wince, but he couldn't really wince because of the cuts at the corners of his eyes. All the flesh on his body ached dully. The mechanical attachment that allowed him to accelerate and brake made his knee stumps chafe and burn. His phantom toes throbbed.

He drove a blue van with cloudscapes painted on the sides. Midway between Fort Collins and Boulder, the wipers slicing clots of snow into icy gruel, his mind set at a low white hum that absorbed much of his pain and most of his memories, he saw the hitchhiker. He appeared demoralized, snow in his hair, his thumb held indefinitely sideways instead of up and out. When the driver eased the van onto the berm fifty yards ahead of him, the bedraggled man began to limp slowly toward the van.

As the hitchhiker slammed the door shut and settled into the passenger seat, the driver put his sunglasses on with his four-fingered left hand, a shallow pink ridge where his thumb had been. His lips, burnt and torn and healed into a dry gape that didn't fit together, wouldn't permit him to smile. He signalled a smile to his brain, and his misshapen lips grimaced. "Hello," he said pleasantly.

" 'Lo. Don't be alarmed, sir. I'm not a serial killer. I just look like one." He blew into his cold hands. He wore a thin colorless cotton jacket and white cotton trousers and white buck shoes without socks.

"I'm not alarmed at all. There's a towel on the back seat and some coffee in the jug."

The driver groaned involuntarily, his trunk shifting under the blanket, as he put the van into gear. He kept his speed at 30 m.p.h. In the thickening snow. There were being swallowed by a prairie whiteout, the distant mountain obliterated, the roadside fields drowned.

"Thank you, kind sir." The hitchhiker drank directly from the thermos jug, gurgling and sighing. "I hope you're not one of those serial killer fellas, givin' me doped coffee, takin' my ears for trophies." He cackled damply.

"Not at all. I scarcely have the energy to kill anyone. Pass me the thermos, I'll have some with you." He drank a swallow of bitter black coffee. When the van slowed, he gave the jug back to the hitchhiker and gripped the wheel with both hands. He wore a brown leather glove on his mutilated right hand.

Thawing out, the hitchhiker cracked a wolfish smile. The storm seemed to amuse him. As the highway iced over, the driver had to pay close attention to driving, but he caught twitches of the passenger's expression. The hitchhiker's joviality unsettled him. In his groin he felt the pressure of urine building.

"I got a hostel in Boulder scoped out." The hitchhiker chuckled and wiped the stubbly strip under his nostrils. The Buddhists put me up for thirty dollars a week. Bunk beds."

"You don't look that rich."

He shimmied with laughter. He wore the blue towel like a loose turban. "Oh, I aint." I was countin' on you t' float me a loan...Sir. What would you say t' that?"

"I'd object to the word 'loan.' It's pitiful and disingenuous. You don't intend to pay me back. It's unlikely you'll ever see me again after today, and if you did you'd scuttle to the other side of the street to avoid me. Now if you just said boldly, 'Give me thirty dollars', I'd probably give it to you. It's not that much money."

The hitchhiker sniggered. "That's pretty good. I don't really need thirty bucks, by the way. I'm way past the point where small sums of money matter. I was just giving you a little teaser. I'd never ask anyone for money in this world. Suppose I asked some unscrupulous person for two bucks. And he says, 'Sure. I'll lend you two bucks, but I want interest. A reasonable interest.' So he slips me the two bucks and I go buy two pancakes and a cup of coffee. My check comes in the mail that day. I cash it and the next day I see the guy, he's dressed the same, he's standin' on the sidewalk waitin' for me. I hand him three dollars and I say, 'Hey, thanks for the loan. Here's a buck interest. Now we're all caught up.' He drops the three bills on the sidewalk. He says, 'Three bucks? Are you insane? The vigorish is $9,998 a day. You're a first-time client, so I'll give you a two-hour extension. I know where you live, my associates are watching your house. I know where your sister lives. In one hour and fifty nine minutes, my people will knock her door down. They'll lift your baby niece out of her crib and nail her to the wall. One heavy railway spike right through the midsection, that's all it takes. They'll take a knife to your sister—first a toe, then a finger, then a foot, then a hand. They're very skilled and methodical characters, my boys. They'll use a hot blade on the stumps so she doesn't get an infection. Don't worry...Then they'll leave sis and they'll go find you. Wherever you've scattered to. Doesn't matter.

You could fly to Cuba or Algeria. We'll follow you, because you're the main source of the problem here. And we like to confront the main source. See? I won't tell you what they might do to you. They have to chase around a lot, they get wired, they get angry. But they're not hotheads or anything. They're not rash. You'll still be alive when they're finished with you. We can't collect from a dead man, and we always collect. Always. Not one default on record. We run our business with absolute efficiency."

The hitchhiker draped the towel over the seat and smoothed his hair. "You see what I'm saying? How the smallest debt could get your ass in an ocean of hot water. Probably never happen, but it could. There are bad people in the world who'd just thrive on the opportunity to sink a man in debt."

The driver slowed to 25 m.p.h., then 20, then found a turnoff. There was a regional bus stop, a small shelter of green tin covering a wooden bench. He rolled to a stop beside the shelter and shut off the engine. They could have been at the bottom of a cold ocean in a school of blind snowfish.

The driver took the thermos and drank more coffee. "Hypothetical misery is like a card game. I was never much interested."

"Sir, I don't traffic in the hypothetical. Such things do happen. Look at this." He unzipped his jacket and tugged his white shirt free, releasing an acrid odor. He jammed the shirt up his back, which was a broad, boiled-pink cicatrix. There were dark healed punctures running diagonally from his shoulder to his waist. "What you see here is your acid, your cigarette lighter, your icepick...Won't show you my legs and feet, they're the worst. Not even the doctors can stand to look at my lower extremities. It's a miracle that I can even hobble around a little bit...You want to t' tell you how I raised the $30,000? It took three days, it was no picnic."

The driver rubbed his eyes. All the windows were snowed over and the air seethed softly. "It's not necessary. I doubt that it would be edifying. Let me tell you a story, just so that we're equal."

"Fair enough."

"I'll tell you why I travel constantly...I grew up in Glassboro, New Jersey. That's outside Philadelphia a little ways. I went to college there, graduated, got married, had a baby daughter. I used all my savings up when our daughter got colic. We were a little short on week and I'd promised my wife to grocery shop. I stopped for coffee in a cafe. I was feeling sorry for myself and I got to talking with this man. He was very professorial and calm and sympathetic. He took out a money clip and gave me two twenties without my asking him directly for a loan. 'Give me fifty a week from today we'll be square,' he said. I was a little nonplussed that he'd charge ten dollars interest, but I agreed to the terms. I was teaching Freshman English at the college and occasionally I took a night janitor shift to make extra cash." He paused and there was a faint sound of leaking liquid in the van.

"Eight days later, I was grading papers at a table in the basement boiler room. I had a little gooseneck lamp. I'd spaced out the loan, I was distracted, I can't really say. Anyhow, two men came down the steps, thump thump thump, on sharp-heeled shoes. 'We're here to pick up Mr. E's fifty. You're already a day late and he's getting cross. Where's the package?' I was puzzled by the odd terminology. 'Mr. E. from the restaurant, you mean? I have his money right here.' I counted out two twenties and a ten. The spokesman wouldn't accept the money. He frowned. 'What's this? Fifty bucks? You owe Mr. E. $50,000.' He was perturbed, but he only raised his voice a fraction. He didn't rant. I shook my head, I thought it was a prank. I smiled."

The hitchhiker nodded minutely over and over.

"You're really putting us out,' the spokesman said. 'We'll have to drown your baby just to show that we're serious. We'll cut your wife up too.' 'This is a sickening prank,' I said. 'Take the fifty dollars to Mr. E. and tell him to see me tomorrow in my office on campus.' 'You're giving us instructions?' he said. I didn't know what to do. They were respectably dressed, not at all like thugs. He was soft-spoken and deadpan serious. The man picked up the three bills from the table, dropped them on the floor, and ground his shoe into them. 'Don't go home tonight if you're squeamish,' he said, and they left together. I thought of calling the campus police, I had an emergency phone right there, but it was so absurd, so embarrassing. They were like mad hatters."

The driver used his gloved hand to massage his forehead and rub his ruined eye sockets. "I finished my shift and walked home. I was tired and light-headed. My wife was bound and gagged on the livingroom floor. They'd slashed her face and her wrists and her throat. Her heart was on the rug. Like a chunk of spoiled meat. I rushed into the bathroom and my daughter was at the bottom of the overflowing tub with a bucketful of cement roped to her ankle...I spent close to four years in an asylum. When I got out, Mr. E.'s men found me in a boarding house in Reading. My wife's parents cashed in all their savings bonds to pay my debt, but it took them several days to deliver the money. Mr. E.'s men started cutting me up on the second day. They have a way of keeping you alert while they're doing it. It's an amazing talent...My wife's parents were very kind. They paid my hospital bills. They bought me this van when I finally got out of the hospital again. It's got 89,000 miles on it now, but it still runs wonderfully."

The hitchhiker wagged his head. "I didn't recognize you. I'm not very good remembering faces. You can believe me or disbelieve me, but I always hated killing people for Mr. E. and he knew where my sisters and brothers lived, you see. He threatened to massacre them all. All my nieces and nephews, too. It all stemmed from a 40 cent loan to make a phone call. I was trapped. I had to work for him endlessly just to pay the interest on my debt. The debt itself I could never pay. It was the same for Billy, my partner. He had a little voice box where Mr. E.'s trooper had burned his vocal chords. That's why he never talked. He had four sons to protect, Billy. He had no choice. Then one day Mr. E. didn't show up for a meeting. We drove to his mansion in a suburb of Philly, cherry trees in bloom, his private tennis court all lit up in the evening. But the house was totally empty. Cleaned out. Billy and I split the money we had and hit the road. They caught up with me, whoever's bunch it was, and maimed me for days on end. Who could I possibly complain to, though? I'd probably killed at least a hundred people myself."

"You killed more than a hundred...Why didn't you get the fifty from the teacher? Everything started to go to hell when we missed that fifty."

"From you? What the hell are you saying? You were locked up in a mental ward. We couldn't get at you."

"From me? Are you crazy, John? Don't you recognize me, is my voice that changed? Hell, they killed the teacher years ago, they laid his debt off on me...Without that fifty I couldn't make my monthly interest to the Pittsburgh people. I lost my status. Your scars are minor, John. Look what they did to me."

He spread his shirt like wings and showed the burnt and gouged and tattooed motto on his chest—PAY YOUR DEBT. He lifted the blanket and revealed the pad beneath his shrunken buttocks, the catheter, the bag of urine, the brace that held his left leg together.

"Mr. E." The hitchhiker whistled through his broken nose. "I knew that you'd find me eventually. Are they following us? When did you see them last?"

"Two days ago in Lawrence, Kansas. I saw a long white car with opaque green windows and Pennsylvania plates. They'll never give up. I owe them $80,000,000. Thereabouts."

"If I killed you and then killed myself, would it be over?"

144

"Never. My family would assume the debt. I'm sure that E.'s men are watching them.

Noise from above vibrated the van. Snow shook loose from the windows. Through a thin frost left on the glass they behold a helicopter descending in a white swirl. It landed twenty feet from the van.

Two men emerged, struggling in the deep snow. They tapped on the side door of the van and the driver slid it open. One man wore headphones, the other a snow-speckled derby.

The man in the derby sat impassively as his partner removed the phones and said, "It's bad. Bad that you'd cut and run on an $87,000,000 debt. We've killed nineteen of your relatives so far, E. Your clan is shrinking. And you still haven't got in touch with Mr. D. A simple phone call, set up a payment plan, what's the hitch? You're callous. Look at the trouble you're causing. You have to get the money. There's no other way. Don't sit in your cozy little blue van and swap lies and rationalizations. You're not part of some saga. You owe money. This is your last chance. Drive to 2600 Wellington Avenue in Denver and see Mr. G. He's quite wealthy and he fancies himself a philanthropist. He funds an orphanage that has over three hundred beds, and it's always full up. Threaten to dynamite the orphanage unless he pays you $88,000,000 at once. The dynamite's in a crate. We'll transfer it to your van. No more lying to hitchhikers now, either. We're batting around up there in the high snow and we have to listen to that nonsense. Just cut it out or we'll tear your tongue off on our next visit. Meet us in Colorado Springs at noon Wednesday. Bring the money to the gymnasium at the Air Force Academy. We'll be on the running track above the basketball court."

In silence they waited for the snow to cease and the plow to clear the roads. They got back on the highway and aimed south, moving in a totally white landscape, a snow-covered wasteland that extended to infinity.

On Wednesday the driver delivered the money in wrapped packs of fifties and hundreds, dragging the two steamer trunks piled on each other in a woden caisson. D. in turn conveyed the money to H. in Amsterdam, and H. sailed by ship to nassau, where he deposited the money and kept it until I. demanded $100,000,000. I. killed H. and used the $94,000,000 he stole from H. to pay J., but since he was $6,000,000 short J.'s men sliced him up with chainsaws and dumped the pieces in a landfill. J. sold his estate and his art collection; sold his daughters to a Kuwait brothelkeeper. He paid off K. and K. went by autobahn as far as he could until L.'s men caught him. By the time that X. received the $380,000,000 it was too late. Y.'s men held him over a washtub and blooded him slowly because he was $8,000,000 and thirty-six hours overdue.

Y. himself was no luckier. Six months later, he made a pilgrimage to Vatican City and they wheeled him up a ramp and into a service elevator and down a long marble corridor as long as a parade route, pink cherubs and silken angels unspooling in endless tapestries for him to peruse with his bruised eyes in his goggling head, and across a crimson rug thick enough to muffle the squeal of his wheels and up to the Pope's throne. Y.'s body, what was left of it, clenched in pain. His metal arms scraped the sides of the wheelchair as he thrashed, or tried to thrash. From burnt lips he whispered, "Your holiness. Please. Tell Me. Z. that I'll get his money I'll pay the debt. I swear."

The Pope's eyes blinked once. He didn't bother to bless or address Y. He thought, "When are those bozos gonna learn? Little kids runnin' around and makin' boom-boom noises. Pretty soon they all grown up and loose in the world. Jackin' each other up, down and sideways. I wash my hands. No use talkin to Z. He don't listen to me, he says I owe him money. Just say your prayers, boys. Say your prayers. 'Cause one day you gonna wake up in a strange place, strange as Madagascar. Blue-black sky. People be shakin' chicken blood on you, dancin' around you, ho-dooin' you. Boy, you gonna wish you said your prayers then. 'Cause I can't help you, God can't help you, not even Z. can help you when you wake up in Madagascar."

NOCTURNES

DR. BERNARD FORCHON

There's an evening breeze beginning. I sit here, slothful in my leather-seated swivel chair, and watch the sky. A pale-pink moon has already risen. In the fading daylight a mob of jungle birds hoots. Over time—months, years—this cacophony has become as familiar and rooted as the chirp of locusts or the rasp of crickets in the backyards of my childhood.

I'll shut my eyes. Doze. Chase the tinctures of memory as the light goes away. The sound of the ocean rolls in, a soft cannonade. Like the birds' screeching, it doesn't jangle me. I'm accustomed to certain kinds of tumult. The cries of birds and beasts, the rustlings of jungle vegetation, the combings of wind, the dramatic colorscope shiftings of sky, the crashings of water—they blend into a violent harmony. Existence in collision, bashing element against element. Yet holding together.

On the ocean horizon the sunset sky spreads. A couple years

ago, from a skiff, I watch three pelicans in formation fly directly into the sundown, each X-rayed in crimson. An odd and dreamy sight. I felt unmoored, as if I were swimming weightlessly in a red pool on Mars. Now, as twilight darkens the jungle and the ocean booms in the distance, I'm suspended for a few moments. Eyes shut. Darkening inside myself, in sympathy with the night. Ebbing, pacified. In a lull between worry and sleep.

Full dark now. I'm yanked back to my history. I'm remembering the dormitory I bunked in during my internship. Buffalo, New York—1956. A homely city, brown and white in winter. My bedroom walls umber, my blanket dusky wool, the floor opaque-brown lacquered wood. The hospital made of dried-blood-colored brick, the fire escapes olive-brown, the dead ivy grayish-brown and scraggly against the first-floor facade. Shelves of snow on the roofs and ledges, heaps of snow as big as igloos in the parking lot. Old boxy Nashes and rust-brown Fords and tan Plymouths.

The interns, those who lasted, were often cynical fellow. Aside from the moony dropouts, we formed a mordant sect. Autopsies were vaudeville. The severest physical injury was nature's black joke. Over and over, we were shown that in the wrong circumstances the human body was as fragile as a flower petal. I had to examine patients who'd shredded like petals in pelting rain. I was just getting my sea legs in the area of human pain—the raw stuff of doctoring—and I needed that tonic cynicism.

I knew the danger of engulfment. Inside me there was a valve that released awe and grief—and I jammed it shut. By force of cynical will. I avoided the eyes of the eight-year-old boy with the suckhole in his narrow chest where a shotgun slug had cored him. I steeled myself to attend the teenage girl who'd been scalped, and her face prismed, by the brunt of a coupe windshield. Gouts of blood didn't faze me. Nor did the various gravies and drools and seepages that come from ravaged bodies, savaged bodies.

I'd give myself pep talks. Goddamnit, I was determined to function. As a mechanic—tinkering with pain, fretting it, diagnosing it, delving into it, outwitting it. Or calmly overseeing its cessation in death. At night, beneath my coarse blanket, I listened to the radiator sputter and the faraway cars churn the snow. I felt like a competent man. Attuned to the noises—the click-squawk-chirr-scrape-rustle—of existence. I slept like an infant usually.

I was assigned to the Burn Ward—we were all rotated through there—and I saw people whose flesh had been baked like pottery in a kiln. I saw new shades of red. Scorch-red. Sear-red. Sunset faces. Scabbed faces. Lips split like grilled sausages. Backs fried to red maps. Patients unable to speak or whimper or gasp. Tube-lubricated, immobilized. As I trod from room to room, I was unnaturally aware of the sound my throat made as I swallowed, trying to flush a thread of wintry phlegm. It was necessary to swallow, to bite back, to clench, to snuff feeling—and I felt this necessity of withdrawal as a contortion inside myself. I was a good, resolute doctor, but I had to hobble myself to remain competent. I've never discussed this with another doctor.

The moon has shed its eerie pink sunset haze and has emerged yellow-white. Faintly pitted and scarred, like old skin. Elegant on their slender poles, the yard lights are all aglow. Moths and smaller bugs tumble around the protuberant bulbs. A shriek makes my skin go to gooseflesh. It's not a bird—it's one of the patients, probably awaking from a dream.

Gina, a nurse's aide who's shy and furtive, brings my dinner on a tray. In the gloom she stands for a moment. She makes an interrogative sound, almost a plea. I nod. Balancing the tray gracefully in one hand, she dips her other hand down and switches on my desk lamp. She tries a swift smile, and she's very touching. The echoes of her gestures hit the walls of my groin. She's olive-skinned, with tendrils of lustrous hair as dark as ebony crepe paper dangling from her bun. When I say "Gracias", the word itself—the lilt of it—seems to please her. Her smile blooms again. She backs up two paces, fidgets. She watches me—like a petite gunfighter, with her big black eyes—as she retreats from the room.

The food hasn't much savor. Baked fish, gluey rice, slices of pale-orange melon. I eat these slippery, sweet devils with my fingers. I turn off the apple-green rectangular lamp and sit in the moonlit room, smoking and musing. Far from my young callowness, far from snow. The geographical tendency of my life-travels is erratically southwestward—from Buffalo to Louisville, Kentucky to St. Louis to Tempe, Arizona and now here to the Villa Por Mar on the Pacific Ocean, halfway between Mazatlan and Tuxpan.

I am responsible for just eighteen patients, most of them wounded and traumatized past human measure. One of my tasks is to devise a system of New Measurements. How much recovery is possible. How slow—almost millenia—the healing often is. How the occasional patient knits his body and psyche back together. Mostly, it's like playing chess with pieces the size of skyscrapers—a long time between moves. I try not to dwell on my frustrations or petty administrative sanfus. I castigate myself severely whenever I fall into a funk.

We all must batten ourselves against daily despair. Self-annihilation, even. It's our occupational risk—nurses, doctors, aides. And myself, the lordly administrator who despises the notion of lordliness. It's almost humorous. To think that the morning maids or the driver who delivers bottled water might find us all one day—raving and hollow-eyed and defeated. The healers gone to ruin.

MARTINA PIZARCZYK

Things that once mattered no longer do. Whether I'm pretty. Or my nose is too sharply tilted, beaky. Or my hair a wiry dirty-blonde that collapses in damp patches in the humidity. Whether the palm of my hand sweats when a boy I'm attracted to holds it—that disparity, to feel soft and agile and cozy in my romantic heart and to be clammy and clumsy and disheveled in the actual motions of life. Whether I'm invited to the dance. Whether there is a dance at all. Polite and social and simpering and far from harm, with paper streamers hanging.

The way I feel now, I'd skip the prom. It's an inappropriate dance. We're tribes, still. We should dance tribal dances. Every town should build a bonfire as big as an amphitheater. All the dancers should wear bone jewelry and shake bone rattles and whoop like monsters.

Sweat trickling down my forehead. Jungle mosquitoes coming in, whining and attacking. It terrifies me—the narrowing of self, the jagged obsessiveness that cuts me. But how can I oppose it? It's right. Proper. Ordained. That I should devote myself to them. Totally. It would make up for everything, it would make me feel as if God Himself had embraced me, if I could pull just one patient back from the brink. Just one.

Every night I do this. Sit here and edge myself out and balance on the brink with them. They cringe, locked in fear. Of everything— me, touch, voice, light, darkness, breeze. To them the soughing of the breeze in the trees may sound like the approach of a fist or club or razor. Someone's coming, they must think.

The hot flood of blood filling my face. My voice, wheedling. "No, no. Darling. There's no danger here. You can heal You can go from .001 to .002 to a thousand. I'll help you, an inch at a time. There's no danger. Do you understand. No peligro aqui." The faint wheeze of his breath. I make lightning prayers. Help me. I'd tear my flesh out in divots, I'd scour my nerve endings with a wire brush, I'd drip acid on my tongue. Just give me the angelic idiom.

No peligro aqui. It's the lie that balks me. There's danger

everywhere. The jungle, the deep ocean, the burning sun, the predatory men in uniforms. It's everywhere.

I'm sweaty and nearly useless. Linguistically hampered. Impaired. Down on the beach, someone's playing music. Maybe dancing barefoot on the cooling sand, amid the scissor-foot crabs. Prom—old Mrs. Scheinmuller, hideously horse-faced, lurking by the punchbowl in her yellow chiffon dress. All the boys with aftershave and erections and cuffed pants and clumpy shoes. My damp hands, my uneasy smile.

My hands are the least of it. I sweat freely now. In the topical afternoon heat, all the nurses do. The sun hangs pale and burning, like a boiled egg in the high humid haze. For all the cooling effect it has, the ocean could be a steambath.

Even though it burns my skin, I use an astringent toilet water. It's in our written guideline not to wear perfume. Not to arouse the patients. Some of them have been wounded—butchered—in the genitals. We are encouraged to be sexless, nurse-wraiths.

How this must please the fire dancers! And what a boon for the manufacturers of catheters, rubber sheets, protective pads. Their stock soaring.

I'm butting the walls of reality again. Can't help it. I could saunter along the beach, dance in the dark to the castanets. I could requisition the van and drive to the cantina and drink silty red wine until I was dizzy. I could bewitch myself, change from a tuning fork to a sponge. Like the earth itself. The soaking blood makes the grass greener, the bones are nutrients for the soil. Infinito muerte. That's the phrase.

In San Francisco, at the convent school, we were given a shock course one day. Slides of male victims The radiant white screen. Then for two or three seconds the hovering color image. Click, and it was snatched back into the slide tray and replaced with another.

A man with his severed scrotum stuffed in his mouth. Click. A man with his eyelids sliced off. Click. A man whose face had been doused in insecticide until it lumped into a gargoyle shape. Click. The nurses—many of us—felt a liquid loosening. Everything that could break loose did—tears, mucus, nosebleeds, drops of pee in our pants.

We drank water, squirmed, rubbed our eyes. Snuffled like cowards. The lecturer cautioned us. She told us not to linger on feelings of pity, horror, helplessness, revenge. That the point of being here was that we could help. That we were troops, an army of another sort.

She described what the soldiers did to women, sometimes, in rebel villages. Rapes. Disembowelments. The most intimate parts taken as trophies, as gewgaws. Hatred discharged as totally as the sting of a hornet. And we—volunteers—were to be a counterweight to that hatred.

The class shrank from two hundred to seventy-five to thirty. For days and weeks, I felt frail and tentative and nearly defenseless. But I stayed. I had to.

To fight the images, I tried to build a pulse in my mind A steady neutral ohhmmm that I could rely on. That would neutralize the sounds conjured by the images. Drilling, cutting, tearing.

Inevitable questions. What about the photographer who took those pictures? Was he humming ohhmmm, ohhmmm as he adjusted his lens? He must've been. And where does it end? What if the afterlife is a great starry vault, with tens of billions of souls, all humming ohhmmm forever?

I doubt—God, myself, everyone.

It's lucky. Tereza comes in. She gives me a chocolate-covered mint wrapped in silver foil. She smiles her blithe, sympathetic smile. After she leaves I peel the chocolate disc from its crinkly wrapper. Put it on my tongue and let my warm spit melt the thin chocolate skin. Delicious seeping mint beneath the dissolving chocolate.

I ignore the big moth that's bumping the porchlight. Even though it's beautiful—maroon and beige and velvet-black. I press my eyelids shut and cruise down the line of cottages mentally. I have to. It's all I have to hold me to the earth.

Hector, blind. I've spoonfed him. Bathed his skin which is wrinkled and striated like a walnut. Talked and crooned to him in my wretched broken Spanish. No response.

Rodolfo, crippled in the legs. He will talk a little, staccato and indecipherable. I smuggle in extra cheese and fruit for him.

Emilio, toothless and lamed and castrated. I linger with him—it's impossible not to. The ohhmmm snaps. He's young, no more than thirty. Even with his puckered face—a dentist will try to fit him with dentures, eventually—he's striking. Like a prince or grandee. A sinewy, fine-drawn handsomeness. He doesn't flinch—visibly. He doesn't curl into himself like a chinch bug, as some patients do. He doesn't speak. His gaze isn't quite level, not quite downcast. Indeterminate.

His eyes are brown. Bending to square the blanket on the bed, I peered below his tilted brows and spied his brown eyes. Looking back at me.

It's an awful memory—what my face must've looked like as I attempted to smile. The heat flashing over my cheeks like an atomic blast. The surfaces of my eyes burning like suns.

EMILIO SAEZ

The opiates they give me are insufficient. The pain plays inside me like a melody. When I move my head, my temple is bitten by pain. My hands shake often—a kind of palsy. My guts gnaw themselves. In my kidneys and groin and anus shots of pain volley. My heart rushes, quickens. Then goes sluggish for a time. It takes up my day, following the caprices of my pain.

I'm thankful that my benefactors—Yankees, Swedes, Mexicans—have provided me with this airy white -washed room. This firm mattress, with a pale-blue blanket and a good feather pillow. This oak table with a cut-glass vase. Wild lilies with waxy-red freckles propped in a sump of water. The smell of the flower-water is not so disagreeable.

I've spent the last two years in rooms. My cell—low ceilinged and webby, mossy stones unevenly mortared, muck on the floor. They would dash water onto the floor, but since there was no drain it would puddle and make a stench, like a lagoon. The color of the stones was brackish, like frog-skin. Flies rock-climbed the walls. Buzzed and muttered. Walked into my earholes and flew out when I slapped at them.

Up the corridor was the interrogation chamber. It was lit by a hard light, or a brightness where pale-yellow grades into white. It was unventilated, smoky, muggy. An oily sweat leaked from everyone's pores. This angered the soldiers. There was a washtub with twenty or thirty gallons of water in it. They dunked me. They flogged me with wet towels. They dislocated my collarbone. They hectored me. They drubbed me with cane sticks. They held a butane lighter to my hands, my feet. They loomed over me, their breath smoky or carious.

Many different ones. Gray shirts, gray trousers. Black boots. Dispassionate or enraged, well-muscled or puny. Young boys with cottonseed mustaches, experienced men with seamed and papery faces. An officer with red epaulets once—he gave me a popsicle, but after I'd licked and eaten part of it he took it away and pitched it in a barrel. They used electricity, too. Two clappers the size of hairbrushes pressed to my chest or my balls.

I had a game. I would say to myself, I am a mule. Trudging in a circular mule-track, doing dull mule-labor. My moans aren't human moans, for human moans become grating and tedious to everyone in the vicinity, even the moaner himself. The sounds I make are mule-moans, brayings. I would daydream, adding each detail reasonably. I posited that I was bound by a harness to a wooden wheel that turned all day long. I was the hand on a mule-clock. Where the harness cinced my hide, I was rubbed raw. My burns and scrapes and gouges were no worse than average mule-wounds Not worth complaining about.

I could not sustain such fancy. In time I was made to admit that a mule feels extraordinary pain. Brays like a riven child. Anguishes. And its braying unites it with other beasts. To the fish with the hook-cut in its mouth, slowly asphyxiating in a bucket. To the wild pig, its eye cloudy and lidded, fallen in the jungle grass with a halo of flies feeding in its blood-slick. To the beef cattle in the abattoir, writhing and slobbering and wishing that they could levitate like angels.

My actual status was borne in on me. I wasn't a mule. I anatomized myself, felt my cuts and scabs. I dipped my finger in impure water and ran it over my lips. Bits of my education flickered in my head—equations and formulae, the woodcut illustrations from volumes of Cervantes and the Bronte sisters. I recalled the sepia drawings of the gaunt man with the spade beard and the lady holding a lantern on a stormy moor. I remembered the odors of the chemistry lab—caustic, foul, invigorating. I dreamed once that huge balloons floated over the ocean and siphoned up the water.

Back to the interrogation place. They slugged me like amatuer boxers. They hit me until their shoulders ached, their hands throbbed. They cursed me for causing them such discomfort. They dunked me in the tub. My lungs were burning-sore and sodden. Then the nonsensical questions. Why were there rifles hidden in the shed behind your house? There's no shed behind my house. I have never kept firearms. The interrogator, lank and archaic like

Quixote, sucked his cigar mournfully. Abruptly he ground the ash into my wrist.

Why is your sister a cohort of the rebel Tengu? What whorishness possessed her? My sister died of pneumonia at age eight. She's buried beneath a lime tree in our father's orchard. Plunged in the brimming tub again. At eye level a waterspider skittered like a paddle-wheel boat.

They quit asking questions. They visited me in my cell. Not on a daily schedule. At scatter times. One held me, embracing my torso. Squeezing the other, wearing mitts made of animal hide, pried open my mouth. They warned me—if I bit, they would haul me out to the courtyard, lynch me upside down, throw gasoline on me, and torch me.

I gaped my mouth. His fingers were so powerful and deft that he didn't need pliers. A taste of mud on the thumb of the mitt, pressed into my gums. Two bunched fingers wobbled an incisor. He grunted, spasmed. With a cry of effort, he tugged out the tooth.

After I sacrificed a couple of teeth, I began to consider the remaining thirty bad, cumbersome. In time they tore them all loose. They snubbed me for two or three months. When they came back for a visit they switched their attraction to my genitals. Rambunctious. Goading each other. Bull-in-a-pasture sport. They teased me, tested me. How much wire, how much steel, how much wood I could tolerate. They pared some skin from my penis.

I was lucky. They didn't covet me, as they did Amerigo. They raped him a number of times. Like boisterous boys at a carnival, hammering a gong. It was sanctioned—he was only seventeen, a stripling. To rape an adult man would be unseemly, degenerate. Not a soldier's act.

It took only a few days to rape Amerigo to death. Likely he was ruptured inside, bleeding like a lake back into himself. They bragged that they didn't bother gouging in the clay to bury him.

They berated him in memory. They complained of blood on their penises, of blood and dung and germs. An infamy that Amerigo should be so lax in his hygiene, that he should bully them. They took revenge by discarding his body outside the compound for the dogs to scavenge.

So. I can remember a few things that happened. Not so many. I am fortunate to be a teacher of mathematics. Not a poet or a balladeer, who would transcribe or singe every note of his human ration of misery. I wouldn't be able to describe everything that's happened to me. Everything I've seen.

I listen to the melody that plays inside me and I know that it will never cease I have given no testimony to my kind keepers. I did speak once, to confound a doctor whose manner nettled me. I didn't like his looks, either—his sticky colorless hair, his freckles and sun-cancers and blemishes like specks on a river rock. I said, "It hurts terribly to piss." He looked to the side of me. His lips pursed, but he was unable to reply. With a few mild, factual words, I had enfeebled him.

And the nurses. They fidget. Bite their lips. Funnel their entire selves into piteous looks. They would pet me like a terrier if I encouraged them. One in particular. Her hair spiky blonde. Her skin a damp pink. Her eyes green. I've peeked and seen her eyes. Normally I let my chin sag. But she bustled, squatted beside me, fiddled with my bedding. So I peeked.

It would be folly to talk to her, for she's the kind who would dig—so gently—the spikes from the wounds of Christ. She would sterilize and dress the ragged pegholes in His hands, the ashes in His feet. She would cradle Him. Sing to Him. Murmur. She would sleep by his pallet like a dog. And if the soldiers in their uniforms came to seize him, she would cry out, "No! Take me instead."

DR. BERNARD FORCHON

I'll stay up all night, dribbling smoke from my pipe. In the moonlit room the pale smoke hangs and drifts and fades as if it were the clouds and my craggy old face the moon. I'd like to be the moon for a change.

It's not so different from sleep—sitting here and dreaming upright, in my stale clothes. Certain vanities have eroded. I don't worry much about my iron-filing stubble, my incipient dewlaps, my aches and pains, my funky leonine scent, my weathered cock drowsing again my thigh. It's what I am now—a sixty-year-old medical functionary, put out to administrative pasture. I haven't operated in six years. Haven't laid so much as a dry flat depressor on a patient's tongue.

Thirty years ago, there was no more than a dash or ellipsis between death and sex. Hemorrhaging accident victim, clamped open for futile surgery. Then a nurse's moist sex, entered. I was a canny and forgetful animal, prowling from one arena to the other. Going from death to orgasm—like a lion. It's how I imagine them, on the savannah. Tearing chunks from a zebra, eating and grumbling. Then a slumber. Dreaming. Then awake for a growly, ravenous mating.

I drink some tepid water, straight from the carafe. I move to the window seat, a cushion set on the marble ledge. The pain that shoots up my back—a grouchy old man's characteristic pain—doesn't seem unjust. If pain must be universally dispersed, I deserve at least this much of it. I let two sour aspirin sit on my tongue for a minute, then swig some more water.

Past the rim of the jungle, in the clearing between the last cottage and the utility shed, I can make out the waves lapping in, their hackles foamy. A patient staggers along the grass. The Samoan yard attendant, burly but very adept and lenient, nudges the patient's

160

elbow and steers him like an errant waltzer and guides him back to his cottage. Locking the cottages at night is not my policy. We've never had an escapee.

I have my regime of worries. Every night I worry about the nurses. If their fortitude is eroding. If the wick of their resolve is burning down. Four of them are virtually rookies. I can't evaluate them yet. I consider the veteran four.

Eileen, with her chunky arms and deep-set dimples and efficient blue eyes, has torque. She could wade into havoc—saving those she could, thumbing shut the eyes of the dead.

LeAnne is fine, too. She has a dreamy displacement that sees her through—a stalwart sleepwalking nurse, one of the ablest varieties.

It's Martina and Tereza who aggravate me.

Tereza is too young—and she's unconsciously flirtatious. I hope it's unconscious. I've talked to her and I don't doubt her commitment, but she exudes a vixenish quality. At a party she would be the woman who magnetizes every cock in the room. I may have to send her back to the States. Ludicrous and unfair, but I'll have to mark her file with the bureaucratic equivalent of TOO CARNAL. But I'm temporizing. I don't enjoy feeling like a shitheel moralist—which is to say, I guess, that I'm unsuited to be an administrator.

I don't question Martina's ability as a nurse. She's neither crafty nor seductive. She's meddlesome. Repeatedly she's probed for addresses of relatives, for biographical information on the patients, for permission to attend the patients when she's off-shift. I've tried to cajole her, to counsel her in the skill of emotional pacing. She nods fervently. She agrees with every dictum. But she continues to overextend herself. She's excessively dedicated—a fanatic.

Last week I said to her, "Martina, what's happened to these men surpasses our ability to deal with them personally. If we make each patient a personal crusade, we'll go loco. As members of the medical community, we must treat them as kindly as we can, but not with personal involvement. It can't work...And I hate the stuffiness and officiousness of this. Believe me, dear, I do. But it's my job to see that you don't lose your way. I know you've studied Spanish, you've filled in and done extra shifts, you've dedicated yourself. But you're doing too much...I can't release information on patients. I can't have you writing letters. It's not a blunt matter— it's delicate. These men's relatives are in danger in many cases. You could jeopardize them, out of misplaced zeal...Please accept it, dear. You have to keep some distance—or the job will swallow you. I need good nurses...this distancing—it's not the same thing as heartlessness. And it's the only method that has much chance of working. If we have nurses becoming entwined with patients, it'll be chaos. We're trying to help these men recover from chaos."

"But they're not, are they?"

Her face, as she spoke evoked chaos. Her agitated green eyes, the sunburn flaking on her nose, her cheeks streaked with emotional heat, her lips quivering. A clotted, beseeching, mad look.

Despite my thirty-five years of experience and all my wiles and my bedrock humane cynicism, I had no comeback. I squeezed her hand. I poured us both a limeade. Martina cupped her glass and drank. When she came up for air, shreds of lime pulp clung to her lower lip.

I don't know what to do about her. My irresoluteness nags me. I have to smile bitterly. Because I no longer know how to tend patients or nurses or myself. I'm half inclined to admit to Martina, "Maybe your way is better. We'll chuck the rules. You be the leader."

MARTINA PIZARCZYK

Theo's huge and smells like a gymnasium. We sit together on the bench under the chinaberry tree, listening to the night sounds.

He wears white pants that are almost phosphorescent. There's a line of hard rubbery belly showing between his belt and the tail of his shrunken T-shirt.

In the last hour we've guided two patients back to their cottages. They tag along the grass, talking to themselves, leaking a little spittle. Stunned to be walking at all, maybe. Emilio has never ventured out at night. I wish, bearing down like a little girl wishing for a pony, that Emilio would limp over and join us.

Theo and I share some Bennies and he's obtained. No sleeping tonight. He gurgles, his wide neck pumping, as he washes the pill down with jug-water. He gives me the jug and I drink too.

Elodie, the night nurse tonight, traipses down the path from cottage to cottage. She carries a lantern that casts a warm, apricot-colored light. Flashlights or penlights can stir terrible memories in the patients, so they're banned. Elodie goes in and out, letting each door thud shut as she leaves. Little concussions. I'm starting to dislike her—she's perfunctory. She's not the sort to linger, to try a lullaby. She has her pile of magazines and her iced cocoa to drink, back at her station in the administrative building.

Theo is tee-heeing and thumping his muscular legs, working up a greeting for Elodie. He's a ruffian-buffoon-flirt. When Elodie exits the last cottage and glances over at us snootily, Theo says something garbled in his Saoan baritone. "Come onna over here, birdy girl. Sip sip."

Elodie is thin, stalky. She has a peculiar sing-song voice that can go from fatigued to snippy in mid-inflection. "Not veez you, fella."

Theo's up off his seat and taunting her, moving like a football player in a practice drill. Arms up combatively, legs trotting sideways in a stutter-step. "Okay, nursey. Missin' all the good things in this life."

Elodie minces back to her station. My blood is popping in my head. Every quarrel or spat or showdown I've ever witnessed or been in myself is layered in my memory. I get up from the bench, fighting vertigo and hyperventilation, and stride over to Theo. He's still doing his drill, his vehement prance.

"Don't tell anybody," I say. I avoid the pathway of crushed stones. I walk on the thick grass that's a luminous yellow-green like corn stalks. I walk toward the black-green grass where the lights are off for the night. Noise penetrates from several planes—the ocean waves breaking, a distant radio from the nurse's quarters, my own heartbeat knocking against my heartwall.

The cottages are set in a horseshoe arrangement along the winding stone path. They're sheltered by trees whose crowns are shaking faintly in the night breeze. A beam of moonlight shines on the gray-green dancing leaves.

At Emilio's cottage I stop. I mop the sweat up into my hopeless hair with my hand. I peer in. I can see his shape on the mattress, which he keeps on the floor now. The custodian has removed the bedsprings and frame, so that Emilio doesn't barge into them. The Benny is buzzing inside me. If I was prudent, I'd hang back and throw block at Theo until I was exhausted enough to sleep.

I know it's wrong, invasive—but I twist the latch. I go in. Set in the wall-plug in the baseboard, there's a tiny heart-shaped night-light. Ten watts of illumination. I kneel beside the mattress. Emilio is awake, his head canted. The pillow has a deep dent in it where his head has squashed it. His shoulders are like a small yoke. His hands go protectively toward his lap like a reflex of prayer. He breathes out, whistles softly through his nose. He's wearing a loose pale gown that could be asylum pajamas or a grandfatherly robe or a tunic.

"I just wanted to see you, Emilio. To see if you were sleeping." I touch his hand, the soft drumstick bulge below his thumb. He slips my grip instantly. As he folds his hands together over his lap, they wobble and vibrate. A thermal current goes through me. My eyes change temperature—sorrowful wet heat.

It's all wrong. A stalemate. To be here, to stay away. To be alive, to leap off a cliff. I need to tell Emilio. My life—everything that I feel and am or long to be—is molten, tearing loose. I need to talk to him.

"Darling—listen. I know that you understand English. I snuck in and looked at your case file. I apologize for being a sneak, but I had to know. The restrictions we're under are wrong. It's not enough to help you dress or wash you or bring you your meals. I know that you agree...I could do more. I could hold you. Just at the shoulders. I know that you're...I could kiss your hands...It's hateful, not to be able to help you more. I know what you feel... When I was a girl, my stepfather would beat me with a strap. For no reason, even. Just for holding an apple. I'd take an apple from the bowl on the table and hold it like a ball—and he'd snatch it away and strap me...It's nothing as bad as what happened to you. It's so much less—but it makes me understand. I feel it...And the girls in the school. They'd pinch me. Spit on me. They were a herd and I was a stray...One time, I put a bobby pin in my eye and scratched the cornea. I figured, if I had to wear an eyepatch I'd be exotic. I'd be intimidating. I'd be this crazy pirate girl...I've never been happy. Not one day in my life. Never. The funniest thing is—I've never slept with a man. I haven't even come close to doing it...I'm all knotted up. I'm all caved in. I'm awkward. I sweat. My nose runs. I get rashes. It...Oh Jesus. It's so little to complain about...I want to help you. I'll do anything. Can't I hold your hand? Mano. Your mano...When I was in San Francisco, I stayed at the guest hostel inside the convent. There was a television in the lobby and one night I watched this program about the Alaskan salmon. How they spawn and swim downstream for hundreds of miles. Flopping down waterfalls. Determined to get home to their part of the river and have their young...there were stone slabs in the shallows, where

165

the bears wade out and catch the salmon. They grab them and bite them in half. Rip them with their claws. Gut them...They gorge themselves until they can't eat any more, but they keep grabbing the salmon anyway. They showed a female salmon, the last one in the program. The bear slashed it open—and its roe spurted out. Then he just pitched it on the rock and it lay there, gasping...The river water was so beautiful. It sparkled. And the clumsy, oafish bears were even endearing...I just sat there in my bathrobe and watched it. I was dazed at the time. But I keep remembering it. That it seemed to sum things up. Life. Everything."

In the warm night air, nearly breezeless, Emilio has tugged the blanket back. On the bare sheet he sits against the wall, his steepled hands over his groin. He rustels a little. Makes small liquid sounds. He regards me.

I nestle on the outer edge of the mattress, in my separate space. The heat is levelling me, burning me down. High in my brain, there's a tiny shelf that hasn't gone molten. And it's warm. Starting to steam.

EMILIO SAEZ

I sleep more in the daylight. Little naps. It's better to wake into surrounding light, ambient light. So that I can tabulate the things in the room. The water basin with its stain of rust that's corroded the enamel. The commode painted a coral-pink. My portable closet, the size of an old-fashioned telephone booth, with my shirts and pants on wooden hangers. My blanket, that was once clean and cotton-smelling but is now imbued with my body odor, the unmistakable stink of my dying body.

Certainly, despite all the care the doctors have lavished on me, I am dying. Not too long ago, I would have welcomed quick death.

I don't believe in Heaven or the passage of souls. Only that there will be a darkness. Neither warm nor cool, neither enormous in dimension nor cramped as a coffin. Just a peaceful darkness. Not even peaceful so much. I think that the contrary notions of peace and strife will no longer obtain. It will be just a darkness, and it will go on forever.

It's strange. Lately, in the last few weeks, I've begun to fear death again. It makes no sense. When I feel the twinges of pain in my shoulder blades, the neuralgic pain that maims my fingers, the pain in my heart that threatens to short-circuit me, the pain of pissing as if my water were hot needles—I conclude, surely death is preferable. But there is something about me now that is like an acquisitive child. I'm childishly eager to put on my clean shirt each morning. Childishly eager to taste the different vegetable and fruit gelatins and baked fish that are served. Childishly eager to listen to the ocean, night and day.

Most nights, I fall into a brief sleep after sundown and wake at eleven or midnight, when the night nurse stops to give me my pills. She talks an odd mix of Spanish, French and English—a Martinique lingo. Tonight I have a second visitor. This unwelcome nurse with her English and hesitant Spanish, who's overdosed herself on her hurts and slight disappointments. Questioning the reasons for our system of pain. Fish and bears and water and air and people and gills and claws and the life leaking from everything in the end. Not so wicked and incomprehensible a system.

I was born into it, as she was. As the men who beat me and burned me and cut off my balls were. I know them well. Born in the poorest villages. Dressed in rags and oily discards and cardboard shields and even woven leafy underpants like pygmies from New Guinea. Lice in their hair, worms in their stomachs. Scrabbling for so much as a scorched tortilla with a dab of cold beans.

As I am enamored of my cotton shirts and clean socks here

at this ocean habitat, so they are enamored of their starched gray uniforms, their water-tight boots, their wonderful guns and bayonets and grenades. The officers told them that all their deprivation previously, all the suffering of their families, was caused by rebel mischief and perfidy. That their sisters who were gone from the village were abducted by rebels. That their meager crops were uprooted by rebels. That their churches were ransacked by rebels.

Absurd to trace the injustices. They are linked in long protein chains. Anyone seeking vengeance would have to trek all the way back to the Creator. Then what? Burst into God's chamber and put a dagger in his chest?

If not a mule, be a salmon. Inevitably plucked and ripped. Eaten or left to putrefy on the sunny rocks. No—I'm through with fancy. I accept being the man I am. Quite useless, untalkative, but breathing and thinking and speculating nevertheless.

Poor grasping girl. She's misunderstood her function. She's a bandage-changer, an elbow-holder, a water-pourer. Nothing more than that. I have no interest left for people. I would be interested if she brought me a snowball from the north, where she originates. I would like to heft a snowball once. She makes familiar noises. Stifled weeping. Incarceration noises. She's weak and aching and confused, like a new prisoner. Unsure of her strange new curriculum.

True night now, the darkest hours. I hear the footsteps coming. Two men in white pants, a doctor and a big orderly. They coax the slipping sack of her body upright. She speaks my name. She moans, though no one has beaten her. She's being flogged from the inside out. Clawed. Chewed.

I have to blink the lids of my eyes shut. Inure myself, as I have done thousands of times. Because I don't want to witness her life's blood, or any phantom embryo she might carry, spray out onto my clean white walls.

MAGNIFICAT

Above the airport at Dar-es-Salaam the sky is vibrant red. The sunset sky is like a lake holding the reflection of a vast tribal fire. Parked along the fence are homely European cars, and a ramshackle, triple--decked bus—a refugee from Piccadilly. His face impassive and as ashen-dark as charcoal, the driver stands beside the behemoth bus and serenely smokes a spicy brown cheroot.

Josie and I slip past a squatting beggar who proffers a bowl of obsidian wood. A lone-legged child hops in a quik fandango, and Josie stops to give him a few notes of paper money. Inside the terminal it is pitilessly hot. A bazaar of vendors and small scurrying men in white shirts and clip-on ties. Arabic, African, European and American bodies mill about. Saffron gowns, lavender gowns, carmine gowns. The tile floor, of ebony and cream diamonds, has an Alice in Wonderland feel, and a pilgrim kneels on one black diamond. Is he praying or groping for something lost?

Josie cocks her head and smiles. Where her blouse opens, her neck and breastbone shine with sweat. She walks in an enthusiastic sashay just ahead of me, her hand reaching back to take mine. Each of us carries one big, knockabout bag—hobo's luggage that belies our modest wealth.

We follow the crowd of bustling strangers up the long, diamond-patterned corridor. Josie fiddles deftly in her handbag, which is looped over her arm, and finds our tickets. I swoon a little in the heat, pricked by the finality of leaving, and pass weak-kneed over a riveted metal plate and through the caterpillar attachment, carpeted with a plum-colored rug remnant, that feeds into the belly of the plane.

We wedge our bags—mine of oxblood naugahyde, Josie's of burnt sienna synthetic cloth—into the overhead bins. Tiny, toneless bells rings. From an unseen source there is a whooshing and gurgling noise, as in a hospital room. I am apprehensive, and Josie puts her warm, dry hand over my dank and tingling hand, and squeezes softly. It is delicious to say nothing, merely to incline toward each other in our cramped seats. We don't kiss. I am afraid that some gall of fear has fouled my tongue. I put a stick of sweet gum in my dry mouth. I stroke Josie's hair.

We are all like children, I think. Awakened from a dream, groping for comfort. It must be our earliest memory, this fearful awakening. I shut my eyes, seething with memory, that could be as trifling as an infant's nightmare or as momentous as the fall of great armies. I am just one frightened, hot, displaced human being, clutching my wife's hand and groping inchoately toward the source of my fear.

Josie reaches to buckle my seatbelt. I open my eyes. As we taxi, I see a caravan of trucks on the horizon. A giraffe's head rides along, lifted on its long neck high above the bed of the trailer. We are gunning, throbbing, racing against the red sky, much lower now and bloodier where it meets the dark plain, bled down to embers.

As safe as we surely are, there is an intolerable surly pressure, as if the plane is disemboweling itself. I shut my wincing eyes and my heart scoots like the machine itself, racing up and out. As we slam into the hot dark sky, faint bells gong all around us again, like a door opening in a celestial market. A panicked ting ting ting ting.

Now my heart shrinks back, pumping in its tight cage, but not so agitated. As we soar higher and higher, I notice shimmying silver liquid on the wind (rain?) and, awesomely far below, phosphorescent whitecaps on the Indian Ocean. I touch Josie's arm, feathering the blonde fuzz on her wrist. Laced across her tanned arm, these hairs are the palest blonde imaginable. Josie turns toward me, green eyes batting, lips slightly smiling, tendrils of long blonde hair drifting down to tickle me. I press my gum into the wall of my cheek. We sway and kiss, my ribs pressed by the armrest.

Then it happens. Some stray bomb of matter, as small as a bird or as big as a missile, thuds against the nose of the plane. Instantly we dip a hundred feet. A stewardess with beautiful baked-clay skin is on her knees, groaning and shaking, little cups of orange juice slicking the aisle around her body. A child, dressed in a silken white robe and a tiny turban, solemn as a Magi, keels into the aisle and pitches toward the cabin as the plane shears downward steeply toward the dark invisible ocean. A few yellow lights sputter and expire. One red light convulses and snaps. In darkness now, cut by flames from the cockpit, we roar down a long funnel of space, swallowed.

Pieces of fuselage spit past the window and thunk off the wing. Something hard bashes my ear and my chaw of gum worms down my throat. I try to embrace Josie, but she's ripped away, fleeing backward up the aisle, splayed across her torn seat. Everyone is shouting. Popping metal sounds grow louder and louder. The plane is like a scalded teakettle exploding.

A body is plastered against me, bellowing. I am bellowing too.

171

Jagged metal teeth, lit by fire, are visible above. As we plummet, I am upside down in my seat, looking in panic at the comet of fire eating along the torso of the torn plane and the dark heavens clotted with clouds racing above the line of fire.

For another long instant I am whole, mourning for Josie with my last kernel of consciousness. We are falling toward the dark, calm water in a fiery tumult. Now the fire, dense with gasoline smoke, skitters across me. I pivot somehow, thrashing. Through a hot membrane I see, finally, the ghostly greenish waves combing aslant the ocean, beckoning to me.

My heart is ripped from its meaty socket and crushed. I am in a greater space of sky, falling still, but gently. Like a parachutist. There is a tensile strangeness—heavy, heavy weightlessness. I am pouring through a nocturnal sky that has many rips of faint blue-white halation, scarves of light like radiant eyebrows. This atmosphere is 360 degrees and bottomless. Memories radiate and pass like flotillas of clouds. Maybe I am the clouds now, instead of the earthbound figure standing, looking up in aspiration, from the floor of my slowly turning, rounded planet.

It was wondrous, but too much to bear. I need to shut my eyes, to float, to reach for Josie with a dream-like ease in the darkness. But I have no eyelids. Sight is continuous. I remember the airport lobby, the slow flow of passengers, my hot incipient fear. I think with the most terrible surge of sorrow that I am the cause of the calamity, that some urge for transfiguration inside me conjured the stone that felled the plane. Then something cracks softly inside whatever it is that I am now. My senses are blended. I drink the cool, dark air. I palpate it, lick it, hear it roaring like music. Josie is inside me, riding on my heartbeat. The tall, somber Arab who sat opposite us in an aisle seat is keening like an exultant bird. The torn child in white silk tumbles with his parents, blue sparks scintillating off their silken gowns. There is more and more visible light.

Josie and I are in a storm of luminous souls. There is a shared joke, a delight, passing among us and making us giddy. It is not at all like what our religion or our fancy told us it would be. We are somewhere else, far outside ourselves or burrowed all the wind in, like novas joyously imploding. Up, down; light, dark; life, death— all are overruled.

In my consciousness there are still mortal pangs. I think of some lazing sea creature, afloat on the water, pierced by a shard of metal. Or of fish steamed in brine by the rain of fire. I think of my parents, sitting in their twin chairs, sore legs propped on ottomans. Both are arthritic. Married for forty-eight years, they are still tender together. My mother will stir with a pained sign and answer the phone and receive the news that her eldest son, so wayward, has been obliterated in an accident. I am the first of her three children to die, the pioneer.

I think, are all the passengers on the flight streaming downward, upward, outward, or did some have wasted souls, defiled souls, blackened souls that were crisped like match-heads in the burning plunge we took? Are some lives slammed shut like tiny earthquakes in the bowels of the planet, their extinguished souls no more than rills of dirt shifting and settling in a huge, dark space?

This grief, impossible to quantify or understand, seeps through me. Miraculously, Josie caresses me. There is a bending band of blonde light that I can see, feel, taste, touch—all at once. There is a feeling of radiant gentleness, as if Josie has grazed my lips with one finger and sent a pleasant shock wave rippling through me. Joined in every sense, we fall.

We are sharing a memory now, eagerly. Pale window-glass and beige carpet in an otherwise bare room. Twilight. The rough beard of pine trees shakes in the mountain wind that flows down the canyon flue. Old blue-white snow in early May. I set up the stereo in our new, furniture-less duplex, and we sit against the white wall in the darkening room, with one car pillow for softness, and listen to the Monteverdi Magnificat. An oceanic surge of massed voices rejoicing.

Now it surges inside us, as we drift in this perpetual benevolent immensity of space. There are millions of raining, singing souls, from every known tribe, and blue-white triangular spirits from other galaxies, and bright blankets of ravening, jubilant souls that spread like jellyfish and originate God knows where, and we are all singing the Magnificat together in one great harmonious surge, as if we still had mouths and voices and heartbeats.

www.ingramcontent.com/pod-product-compliance
Lightning Source LLC
Chambersburg PA
CBHW020652260626
47157CB00008B/3005